NOT THAT DEEP

Splash and tell paddleboard adventure on London's canals

NICOLA BAIRD

Cover design: Andrew Chapman

Copyright © 2024 Nicola Baird

All rights reserved

ISBN: 9798877963177

To everyone who loves clean water, plus special hugs to paddle-weary Pete and paddle fans Lola, Nell & Vulcan.

CONTENTS

	Acknowledgments	i
1	Let the best paddler win	1
2	Catastrophe	10
3	Just stay safe	21
4	Of mice and men	31
5	At the *Buddleia* Narrowboat Cafe	37
6	Sunset tour	45
7	Hen party	54
8	Coach crush	63
9	Peace on the water	72
10	Litter pick	82
11	Back at the *Buddleia* Narrowboat Cafe	90
12	Fancy dress litter pick	98
13	You could walk across the canal	107
14	Storm light	115
15	Awkward tour	129
16	Only joking at the *Buddleia* Narrowboat Cafe	139

17	Let's get this festival started	145
18	Trashspiration	155
19	*Wholly Shit Show*	162
20	Crisis at the *Buddleia* Narrowboat Cafe	167
21	Lock less monster	175
22	Not a ripple disturbs the water	185
	Book group discussion starters	190
	More books by Nicola Baird	192

ACKNOWLEDGMENTS

When I began to SUP regularly it felt lonely. Gradually, I met people who also love to paddleboard. That's why this book is offered with thanks to stand-up paddleboard friends I've made through time on the water with Active 360, Bray Lake, Castle Canoe Club, SUP Facebook groups, Herts Young Mariners Base (HYMB), Islington Boat Club, Laburnum Boat Club, Lake District Paddleboarding, Moo Canoes, Paddleboarding London, Paddle Cabin, Pirate Castle Boat Club, Rosie Markwick Yoga, #ShePaddles ambassadors 2024, sup at islington, Ullswater Paddleboarding and Wake Up Docklands.

All have taught me a lot about paddleboarding and also offered fun, work, learning and some fabulous paddles.

A special thank you is due to Rachel Cooke, Jill Nicholson, Lola May, Pete May and Holly Pye for thoughtful reading of early drafts.

Waterways in the UK are lucky to have champions – especially campaign/special interest groups like Paddle UK (formerly British Canoeing) and the Canal & River Trust.

I'd also like to give a big shout out to anyone who has ever rescued litter, in particular the volunteers on the Regent's Canal, plus Lower Regent's Coalition and Planet Patrol.

This story is fiction so no characters (with the exception of Holly Pye) and no incidents are based on any real people or events.

1. LET THE BEST PADDLER WIN

Meet the Boat Club crew: Lara, Flame (who runs #OutdoorSisters), Jack, Ellie, Gladys and Dizzy

And then I fell with a horrible sideways crash into the canal. To be fair Flame had just offered me the most exciting project of my life - which for 54-year-old me was a happy shock. I was also standing on something resembling a flimsy ironing board on the water. But it was my own celebratory punch that tipped me into the chilly water.

My buoyancy aid pinged me up, but I'd still managed to sink deep enough to emerge covered in green canal slime. At least I'd avoided getting a foot stuck in a rusting motorbike or whatever other nastiness still resided at the bottom, despite our constant litter picking.

"You really think I can do this? I mean I've only really paddleboarded here on this canal," I shout up at Flame, spitting out the lentil-shaped duckweed.

I'm not sure Flame heard me. In fact, I'm not sure she could hear me while perfectly balanced upside down on her board. Because she's such a fast stand-up paddleboarder and busy yoga teacher, this *shirshasana* (ie, upside down) is about the only position I can catch up with her for a conversation, otherwise everything's via WhatsUp messages. But if she moves into the *shavasana* (the sleeping pose) I've been warned never again to shout "Are you alright?", else I'll be the corpse.

Flame didn't need to tell me that was a conversational red flag after I saw the fury in her eyes, last September, when Jack powered the rescue boat over only to capsize everyone in her before-breakfast yoga class. He then dosed them in a diesel-stinking wash. As the ladies weren't wearing buoyancy aids, or expecting to tip into the canal before they went off to work, the next ten minutes saw tears (two of the yogies) and apologies (me to everyone) as it was all my fault. Passing by on an early morning bike ride I saw the yoga people had conked out, so it was me who'd rattled the Boat Club's big gates and, really panicking, begged Jack to launch the rescue boat.

Now that I know Jack better, I think he knew all along that there was no problem at all. But he just couldn't resist causing chaos. He denies this of course.

To be fair to me I'd gone past the little park, near the Boat Club, to see mist steaming off the water and nine unconscious people on paddleboards. Back then I was convinced that the canal was a filthy cesspit, as likely to make a group of yoga fans fall unconscious from a miasma of pollutants as gift swimmers amoebic dysentery, but apparently it's just an autumn thing. Water steams.

To apologise to yoga leader Flame, I booked a paddleboard session and to my surprise loved it, and so then booked a tour. After paddleboarding (or as I now say, SUP, which is how those in the know refer to stand-up paddleboarding) once or twice a week for six months through the autumn and chilly winter, Flame encouraged me to try for some qualifications. My husband, Greg, complains that I've ended up a touch obsessed. He still gets confused when I say "I'm off to SUP", because for him to SUP can only be to savour a pint of beer, preferably with his football friends. I've never found a sport I've liked before, but paddleboarding is just such a fun thing to do. Although I still don't like my head going fully under the water as it's not good for the dye.

But let's paddle back to today, 3 July.

I'm in the water thanks to an unexpected, dream job offer. With her thick (real) blonde hair Flame may look gentle, but over the winter I've learnt that this is just a disguise. She can fend off a hissing swan, carry two 12 foot six inch paddleboards and message five of her group chats on WhatsUp – all at the same time.

And in the headstand, she can talk fine. "I figured your age would be a bonus, as you've usually got lots of good sense," she says thoughtfully, "but I've also mentioned this opportunity to Jack as well – you know him from here. And my friend Ellie and another one – there are four of you who might be suitable. Anyway, I'm going to give you all three months to figure out your plans, write up your business vision, demo the hard work to me and then I'll step back and hand my SUP baby over." She stops talking to exhale, or maybe inhale, I'm never sure quite how yoga works. And then opens her eyes. Seeing me green, wet and now almost at her eye level, as only my head is not under water, she visibly shudders.

"Lara, what are you doing swimming in that green patch? It's a lot cleaner away from Swan Island!"

She's right of course, but I'm excited enough to tell a white lie, fingers crossed, as now she really has to believe I'm more competent than I perhaps am with less than a year of paddle experience (and almost all of that paddling a couple of metres behind her). I have a business to win.

"Celebrating," I say firmly and then attempt to pull myself back on to my paddleboard with some grace. I swear this is not possible, so unlucky Flame – if she keeps her eyes open – will have had a grandstand view of old lady me (well, not really, as I've said, I'm 54 and isn't being 50 the new 37?) disguised as a paddlesports instructor (well Paddle UK Level 1) who she'd just suggested had enough good sense to take over her SUP business, dragging herself and bits of green duckweed very inelegantly back on to a bright orange paddleboard. I know she's not going to like this aesthetic.

"Slime does make the sides slippery," I manage to gasp, wriggling most of myself out of the water.

"Om," agrees Flame, making a micro–adjustment to one of the core muscles that I cannot name, nor ever expect to develop. I love the way she can stay upside down in any pose, on her board, on the water, for at least 10 minutes or until certain that the passers-by on the canal's towpath have time to frame a decent pic and upload it to Instagram. This is apparently good for business, especially if they tag it #OutdoorSisters.

#OutdoorSisters is Flame's business of one-to-one paddleboarding, hen party bonding and the SUP club which sees her coaching crew (of which I am a team member) escorting new and experienced paddleboarders up and down Regent's Canal during the summer.

Topped up with canal water I feel an unusual desire to take these business responsibilities on myself. It's not about the money. #OutdoorSisters is a social enterprise and our profits go to the Boat Club to use for any charitable activities, so the coaches get paid the London living wage, which isn't much for a job that doesn't guarantee winter work. It's more a sudden realisation that I really want to take the gifts the gods (well, Flame and the canal) provide, and run my own paddleboard business. It's the right thing for me, I can feel that.

There's definitely something strange in our canal water today: *l'eau d'opportunity*.

Until Flame's chat about the future – it seems she's leaving to focus on being a dog parent and run yoga retreats – I'd been perfectly content to do a bit of freelance paddle tour guiding for fun. Now I am next-in-line, or would be if she hadn't also offered her business to so many other people. So, how can I prove that I'm the right woman? This will need my full attention, and as luck would have it when I shed my wet clothes Gladys the Boat Club cleaner and her daughter Dizzy are in the changing rooms tackling the toilets. Gladys will know what's going on – she even heard that I'd been made redundant from the council where I'd spent 25 years chasing government funding for youth projects in the borough. Every year the job got harder, the feedback more rigorous, the sums shrank and the need grew.

"Congratulations," Gladys had said, shaking my hand when she bumped into me at Sainsbury's after a couple of months of not seeing each other (we used to be neighbours). "You are now a rich woman and no longer need to work for grey hairs! The Lord has blessed you."

I remember that conversation so clearly, with me holding a shopping basket of own brand muesli, discounted leeks and hair removal strips. I answered slowly, as if speaking to an idiot, but the idiot was me. Why hadn't I paid more attention to our Union workplace warnings?

Putting my shopping basket on the floor I remember saying: "Well, I don't feel very blessed Gladys. I'm on a zero hours' contract, so each year I have to sign a 'new' contract. On paper the council says I've been working for them since 1 January this year. So, they've made sure there's no redundancy payment for each year I've worked here. If there was a redundancy deal I'd be getting payment for 25 years of wearing their lanyard and thinking I'm on the council team. The Union is fighting a few cases, and I may be one of those, but I don't feel that's really fair seeing as I never was a UNISON member. If only I'd realised what was going to happen, I'd definitely have joined."

Gladys tuts. "So, you haven't taken voluntary redundancy, with a fat goodbye cheque?"

"No, I'll get about six weeks' pay and then who knows?" I said, starting to cry because, put like this, I've really let my employer mess up my life.

Gladys bear-hugged me and told me to come and work at the Boat Club, where it's friendly and the pay comes weekly. "You know how to paddle, you're paddling with Flame all the time, it's time now to go teach, girl!" She has been there herself for years, maybe not since Day One as the club's just celebrated its 50th birthday, but a long, long time. Paddlesports fans usually come through the youth club, qualify and then go, but not Gladys. Actually I suspect her daughter Dizzy, now in her 20s, has been at the Boat Club since babyhood. I remember Gladys going off to a cleaning job with her little baby on her back. Grown-up Dizzy is rather an enigma to me as she's invariably lost to music, which she plays through giant yellow headphones permanently clamped to her ears. But she loves her mum.

We all love her mum: Gladys is fun at the club. She talks about bus routes with the travel bores and her Trinidadian heritage with all the foodies, and alongside being a full-time cleaner is a fashionista who invariably dresses smarter than the other Boat Club staff who tend to wear over-sized trackies and windproof cagoules on, or off, the water. She also changes her hairstyle every few months. Today she's working it in slick braids setting off her just about wrinkle-free smile. Along with her beauty Gladys has brains, so all the Boat Club staff tend to use her as an agony aunt. That's why I need her help now, while she's trapped changing the toilet paper.

"I'm in a competition that I think I want to win, but I'm not sure who are the competitors," I say in her general direction as I emerge from the shower cubicle half-dressed in a spare T-shirt and a striped beach towel borrowed from the lost property box. It's not the nicest of towels, but it is at least large enough to avoid parading my wet torso.

Gladys nods in sympathy, possibly. She can be a bit of a Sphinx.

"What do you think I should do?" I ask – older women always have good advice. I suppose that might be a myth but recently I've decided it has to be true.

"That's simple my dear, you just get to know all the competitors," says Gladys, adding a giant wink for emphasis.

I like it! Years ago, when I was giving birth to my eldest child – I've got two grown up daughters but neither live at home now – the hospital midwife told me to just "take good advice" when out and about with my newborn. I had no idea what she meant until people started coming over to the buggy, leaning in, and telling me what to do. Socks as gloves was a definite good idea. Dressing a baby in pink so everyone could tell she was a girl seemed a bit less useful. Being told at the library to only breastfeed in toilets was definitely bad. Eventually I had a Top 10 of what might be good advice, but of course the sleepless nights babies specialise in providing meant that I generally forgot what I was supposed to be looking out for. Fast forward 25 years and I reckon I can remember nothing more than "just take good advice".

Gladys has definitely shared some good advice.

"Thank you!" I gush, giving her a hug, rather forgetting that I'm still damp while she's dressed up gorgeously for someone cleaning a Boat Club's toilets – tight red top and a sequin silver skirt. Plus that hair.

"Are you going out?" I ask nosily.

"Maybe," she says sneezing as she squirts sweet-smelling blue gunk around one of the toilet rims.

I think Gladys has a date. That is interesting. Though I hope they'll forgive her choice of perfume.

I pull on dry clothes as modestly as I can beneath the borrowed towel. Luckily I always pack spare clothing, just in case I fall in, though the last time I got wet paddleboarding must have been about three months ago. It was early April, and the Easter school holidays. Flame had agreed to let the kids use the paddleboards as long as one of the team gave them a learning to fall session. Long story short, that person ended up being me.

But before I'd even got the group on the water I managed to trip over a kayak and tumble into the canal. No harm done, except the session ended up being very cold – I doubt the kids could understand what I was saying through my chattering teeth. Now it's July and the canal water is more like a warm bath. There have been so many hot days this summer that the Canal & River Trust have put out a warning that the monster terrapins who spend the summer sun-basking by the canal may manage to successfully hatch their eggs. The Canal & River Trust do not think this will be good for nature.

As Gladys is still busy with the toilets I don't like to ask more about her date, so I try to get her chatting again, but she ignores my questions. Perhaps she isn't in the mood to talk, or maybe she's put off sharing family business given that daughter Dizzy is also in this room, sitting on the bench, eyes shut, feet tapping. She's like security, keeping her mum company at the Boat Club but with her head always in a different space – RnB rather than RNLI. I'm not sure I've seen Dizzy without headphones, she doesn't seem to use the boats and I'm certain I've never chatted at any length to her. All I know is that she's just left university.

Left to my own thoughts I consider all the people Flame thinks might be right to run her paddleboarding business. Can I work out how to knock them off track (or at least their boards) by the end of the summer. Or sooner maybe? I'm sure I need this bit of good job luck more than Jack, Ellie and the other one.

Dried and dressed I go to the pontoon and give Flame a wave goodbye. I'm not sure she sees as she's back on the water doing intense SUP yoga moves with someone I don't know. The woman looks a bit like her – slim, bendy, focused – and even from here I can see she's wearing full Sweaty Betty. It's possible another brand ambassador has popped in for a photo shoot or maybe that other SUP yoga person is Ellie. I take a 30 second video so I can study 'Ellie's' technique, and style, away from the boat club. It feels a bit sneaky, but that was surely exactly what Gladys was suggesting.

2. CATASTROPHE

Lara takes a lift with Jack

My stomach rumbles furiously as I unlock my bike from the bike stand beside the Boat Club's huge gates. Although they are hard to unlock I've always loved the life-size ship's wheel that is set within the metal bars. Everyone gets distracted by them and sometimes American and Japanese tourists following a London walking guide will crowd around to take photos of our gates.

Everyone's on a journey these days except my battered bike, probably because it looks so cruddy that no one steals it (locked or unlocked). One thing's certain, if I get to run Flame's stand-up paddleboard business, or as Jack says, "SUP" (he does love an acronym), then I'm going to celebrate by getting a bike that will whizz me to the Boat Club (actually, anywhere) faster. With this unexpected new business dream I'm going to need plans. My first one is to get home and treat myself to peanut butter on toast and a victory cup of tea. At least that was until I noticed my back bike tyre is flat. Annoying.

"So, how's paddling? It seems like it's been keeping you sup-risingly busy and away from the workshop and all our bike tools," a loud voice says cheerfully behind me. I hadn't realised Jack was at the Boat Club today. But he seems to come in most days, always on different wheels which he's usually doing up. Today's model is an ancient orange MG car with its canvas top rolled down. Over the revved-up engine his voice is still easy to hear, practice from booming at kids on the water no doubt. He must have laser eye vision too, given that he'd noticed the bike's flat tyre.

Jack is my main rival for Flame's paddleboard business. Apart from Ellie and the other one… I bet they all look the part too. Jack for instance is permanently showing off new items of branded Palm, Gill Marine and Hummel gear, worn over baggy shorts whatever the weather, "Because it's half price for Paddle UK coaches and leaders," as he's mentioned to me each time that I untruthfully admire a new bit of his sartorial kit such as yachting cap, free-draining river shoes, Polo shirt. Gladys has never said this, but I'm sure our resident fashion expert would agree that balding, middle aged, middling-build white blokes probably do need to make a bit of effort on the clothes front.

I've also heard Flame say that Ellie is an ambassador for super-pricey (and very chic) stuff, but maybe she was trying to make me feel better about kitting myself up in my daughters' unused grey school trackie bottoms with a hodgepodge of Decathlon sale items. There doesn't seem much point looking too good on the water if people then assume me to be super skilled and expect to be rescued properly. I'd rather they thought I was skint than had all the gear only to discover I've got a very limited idea about how to do the rescue bit and CPR if it should ever be needed.

Clothes might be one way to guess people's abilities, but what I really need to know is how serious Jack is about taking over #OutdoorSisters, given that he seems to spend a lot of time at the Boat Club and is a paddle obsessive.

The first time I ever went through the big metal gates of the Boat Club – if you remember I was panicking that Flame and her yoga clients were all dead on their boards

– it was Jack who was there. As I panicked and shouted for help, he slithered out from an upturned big green canoe, which he was presumably fixing, to listen politely to my hysterical message. I'm normally so sensible, I don't know why I was acting crazy that day, but then again I was in shock at seeing nine 'dead' bodies. Nine! Jack was like a calm hero, telling me he'd take the power boat out to check the situation whilst simultaneously unlocking the defib box and a first aid kit on the wall of a big houseboat moored near the pontoon. Judging by the hand-painted sign above the cabin door this seemed to function as the Boat Club's 'orifice', surely a typo or youth club graffiti?

As he powered up the basin to 'rescue' the women (probably howling with laughter as he went), I found time had stopped still. Instead of peering through the gate to a waterside rail of drying red and green buoyancy aids, towards what I thought were yoga corpses, I tried to steady my breath and pounding heart by studying the local environment. I tried to focus on the Boat Club's collection of shipping containers, painted in a bright yellow probably visible from the moon, where the boats get stored. There's also a brick wash/toilet block for showering. Yes it looked a bit scruffy, but there was a cosy feel too as a couple of old orange kayaks had been planted up with a riot of runner beans and sunflowers. Even in that moment of crisis I noticed the old boat steering wheel incorporated into the gate and the friendly messages welcoming people to the club pinned up on a noticeboard.

It's funny how things work out. If I hadn't made such a daft "they look dead to me" mistake I'd never have tried paddleboarding, or be here now with a chance to run #OutdoorSisters.

But if I want to ooze confidence as the "Flame in waiting", it's important that Jack doesn't discover any more of my limitations. For instance I've no clue how to fix my bike (that's what bike shops are for isn't it?). He also need not find out that I don't know how to repair any part of a SUP board. Instead of letting my self-confidence nose-dive, I sternly remind myself that Flame didn't want a mechanic to take on her business, she just wants someone to get on with the clients so they book again. I can do that!

Trying to stay cool I bluster, "Good to see you, Jack. And you've got another fancy car. Would you…" but before I've even thought up any sensible or distracting question, his phone has rung and he's focused on something else.

I might as well bump my bike to the cycle repair shop on the way home. But just as I'm passing his posh car Jack gestures for me to put the bike in. I gawp. "There's no way that will fit!"

Jack rings off and then starts to laugh. "Of course not, it's a car, an MG Midget to be precise. There's hardly room for me, I'm six foot you know.

"Ha ha," I say weakly, because he's definitely not that tall. Also I'm trying to squeeze my bike between the car and the locked gate without damaging anything.

"Oh, where's your sense of humour Captain Zara? Tell you what, wheel your bike into the workshop and I can fix it when I've got time tomorrow, then hop into the car and I'll drive you to Finsbury Park, if that's where you still live? Always good to double check."

"It's Lara," I correct him. Men always muddle up my name.

It's odd that he knows where my home is, but I suppose Jack is the man with the club's database. There's a lot to worry about: if I take this lift, will he still have time to sort out the flat tyre? And will my growling stomach keep quiet on a short drive? It just looks so unprofessional being ravenous. But accepting the lift solves one problem at least – my out of action bike.

"Not that I know exactly where you live," Jack adds with a fake 'hands together' gesture as if in prayerful apology, it's just that I'm going over to the West Reservoir to meet Ellie and FPK – Finsbury Park – is on the way."

"Oh, do you know Ellie well?" I ask as casually as possible, glancing at my watch as if I'm running late. Taking a lift might be a good move in the circumstances. I might even persuade him to look at that little sneaky video I filmed earlier and tell me if that's Ellie in it.

Jack doesn't answer as he's too busy jangling keys, grinding gears and getting out of the narrow-gated yard. He's one of those noisy men who take up too much space so the MG seems an odd choice. Even if the bonnet of his MG is huge, the passenger seat is tiny. I wriggle myself in and then squeeze my over-full bike pannier on top of my knees. Getting hold of my phone while we're driving is going to be a battle.

"How did you end up with this particular car then?" I ask a few streets later after giving up pushing my wind-excited hair out of my mouth. That's why women in the old days wore head scarves, just in case she got a lift in a passing MG. I'd rather talk about Ellie, but it feels a bit pushy given that he didn't take the hint when I first asked.

Unnervingly Jack puts his foot down on the accelerator hard. He also turns to look at me when he speaks. If only drivers looked at the roads more. And obeyed the speed limit. I'm only half listening to his answer as I try to find a bit of seat, or door, to which I can grip tightly for what is surely going to be a furiously quick journey. Thankfully the back street speed limit is

20 mph, so at least no one else will be going fast enough for us to have a head on showdown.

"I was on the internet trying to buy photos of Great British Sports Cars, put in a bid for £36 and accidentally bought a real car," he says laughing. With Jack it's hard to know if he's joking. "But truthfully MGs are super cheap at the moment as they're unfashionable fuel guzzlers and a nightmare to fix up and run. I'll be selling this one on soon as my motorbike is far better for getting around London. But do you know that vintage sports cars…" He stops talking to brake sharply as a white flash of cat crosses the road by the Japanese noodle shop. But it's too late, the poor animal's clearly been knocked hard by the MG's low front bumper.

"Why did that cat cross the road sideways," yells Jack irrationally as he pulls up by the curb. "On the river you have to go at a 90 degree angle, that way you cross the danger zone quicker and other users can see what's going on. It didn't give itself a chance."

"Jack, that's not really the point, this is a road," I mutter. Checking from the car door I can see that the unlucky animal is under the car. "If you drive back, we can take it to the vet in Cross Street, which is very close," I suggest.

Jack says he heard me say 'drive back'. Basically, he doesn't stay put, or get out and check what's happened. Instead, he reverses with a jolty thump completely squashing the cat. If it wasn't dead before, it certainly is now. I don't want to get out to look at the blood and gore, and I'm crying so much that seeing might not be possible anyway.

And then we hear three siren blasts and realise that all the kids from Islington Academy are about to exit their school day into a cat bloodbath. "You've got to stay parked where you are and not drive anywhere now," I tell him, gripping the passenger seat as if it had brakes, and starting to cry. "The kids won't be able to see what's happened that way. At least let's not upset them."

Jack turns the engine off and there is a horrible silence punctuated by my sobs. Worse, the kids are starting to leave the main building. "We have to look normal if we don't want to upset the children with a poor squashed kitty cat," Jack says slowly as if he's trying to understand what I mean. He hands me a tissue. "Let's just keep talking."

Oh no it's up to me.

After blowing my nose, I manage to stammer out, "How's your paddleboarding?" as the first surge of navy blazer-wearing teenagers walk past.

"Sup-tle! I knew you'd ask that after Flame so kindly put her business into a winner gets it all game," says Jack simultaneously bemoaning the old car's lack of radio because, "We'd definitely look less obvious if we had Capital Radio switched on."

"Well it's something to talk about isn't it? I'm just trying to make us look like a normal broken-down couple," I snap. Hastily adding, "No that's not what I meant," when Jack turns to give me a pretend loving look. I divert myself with a task by struggling to fish out my phone and play a bit of bland pop like any "normal" car passenger bored by their vehicle being stuck in traffic. But I'm sure the kids are going to sense tension in this fancy orange car. They're going to come up close and talk to us. Far worse, they're going to see cat carnage, though I suppose it's possible the cat isn't dead, I mean I haven't actually checked a second time.

"Go on then, Jack, tell me more about yourself," I say reluctantly. He can't resist.

"Well as Flame knows I'm all about stand-up paddleboarding now, kayaks just aren't as fun. SUP is just so sup-erior! Last weekend I went to watch the APP world tour at Canary Wharf. Wow those guys are supersonic fast running up and down their boards. And they churn up the water with their paddles, really dig in. Saw Connell Campbell do his famous turns on the Starboard. He trains in Maui. You know. Hawai'i," says Jack, making it clear in a couple of loudly-spoken sentences that he is far, far better at paddleboarding than I am, and more worldly, considering the accent he puts on to say 'Hawai'i'. I literally have no idea what he's talking about, apart from knowing how to get to Canary Wharf on public transport.

I'm not sure I'm much of a fan of his SUP puns either.

What I've learnt from this short journey, so far, is that in this battle for Flame's business, he's not to be trusted. But Jack doesn't notice my attention wandering... Now he's talking about paddleboarding, it seems he cannot stop.

"And I've just signed up a brilliant PT to get me fit so I can enter the 11 Cities in September. I'm hoping that paddling with clients will keep my basic fitness up and then the PT can push me into new zones."

He witters on. Eventually I ask: "What's PT and the 11 Cities?", hoping the question drowns out my rumbling belly. It doesn't feel good knowing so little or acting out 'earnest couple' chatting in the car as a way of distracting kids from a cat corpse. Being hungry is just an added embarrassment.

"What's that grumbling noise? Do you think that cat's actually alive?" asks Jack leaning forward. I know he's heard my belly talk. He's grinning, no doubt having also clocked my lack of paddleboarding knowledge. Although to be fair to me I'm a quick learner and I can make a mean Excel spreadsheet to track income or coaching hours and I've never forgotten to ask clients to sign their waivers.

Jack is loving this game.

"Only joking. Of course it's dead, I felt a horrible squish and I just hope my chassis isn't damaged. But actually I wasn't going to mention that I've got some food with me that we could eat because it felt a bit off. But as you seem to be starving, there are fresh bagels and a box of French Fancy cakes in that bag by your feet, assuming you haven't trodden on them. You can help yourself and then maybe pass me something while we wait for all these kids to walk on by."

Hating myself I fumble for the bagels.

"Right-i-o, let me summarise what I've heard from you Captain Lara. You don't know what a PT is, well that's a physical trainer, like a coach. And the 11 Cities is this really cool, non-stop endurance race in the Netherlands. It takes five days to paddle around Friesland along the canals. It used to be a skating thing, but since ice started to be rare the paddleboarders have taken over. It's a beast to do when the wind gets up so you need to train with a faster, stronger heartbeat!"

"How many miles do you paddle?" I ask trying to figure out the distances between London, Oxford, Birmingham, Coventry – or what route you'd have to go in the UK to reach 11 cities on a paddleboard – at the same time as the rights and wrongs of eating a truly delicious bagel in a car that's just caused a pet to perish.

A day spent working on the water means that hunger wins out.

"Well, I'm younger than you, so I think in kilometres. Ha! Only joking, 136 miles in five days," he says. Up close his teeth are oddly yellow now he's chewing a halloumi bagel.

"You mentioned Ellie earlier, but have you met her yet?" he says with a rather wistful smile. "She's a phenomenon. Can do everything we can, and then some. She paid for her sports and nutrition degree by modelling, then got into mysticism, ecstatic dance and yoga while competing, as a way of chilling out. And now she runs an occasional clinic at the West Reservoir – tailoring your exact nutritional needs with punishing training sessions and a thick schedule of events. She's funny too and it doesn't half help my motivation that she looks good, but don't tell her, or Flame, I said that, will you?" he adds, gurning those yellow teeth at me. "Because these days good personal trainers – who, remember, call themselves PTs – are willing to sack their clients."

I really don't like Jack, even when he's spilling the beans.

"Will you have time to do much paddleboarding at the Boat Club if you've got all these endurance race plans?" I ponder hopefully, but before he can answer there's a group of the blazer-wearing teenagers surrounding the MG.

"Sir, Miss, there's a Tesco's bag stuck under your car."

"Do you want some help getting it out?"

"Have you broken down or are you pervs hobnobbing outside school?"

"What a cool car!"

"Is that cat dead!?"

"...Did you kill Snowdrop?!"

The sudden plethora of voices make it clear that our plan of pretending ignorance is not working.

I've no idea how to respond to the kids or what seems to be a worried, besuited teacher coming towards us hastily. Even over-confident Jack looks spooked by her. He checks the mirror, adjusts his sunnies, then turns the ignition key, guns the accelerator and we're off leaving Schrodinger's cat, an exhaust trail and tyre burn. A speed camera and then a Low Traffic Neighbourhood camera click as he turns on to Essex Road.

Ten minutes later I say thank you politely when he drops me at Finsbury Park, instantly regretting that I forgot to show him that video clip.

It's not until I'm indoors hanging up my wet kit that I realise even if in the eyes of the law it was Jack who ran over the poor cat, in the eyes of those kids I'm just as guilty. This is something I really don't want Flame to ever find out about. Even if she's more of a dog person.

3. JUST STAY SAFE

Lara and Flame paddle with clients Karen, Louise, Kalani, Ms L

"So, Lara love, I'm going to observe your session today," explains Flame the following weekend when I arrive at the Boat Club on my nicely fixed bike. "I just want you to show me how you're safe on the water with clients. Don't think of this as a big test, because it's not. It's more me paying attention to your chakra and water reading skills. Just do what you normally do."

Normally I'd pull a face and spend the next few minutes calling my paddle 'Chakra', but as Flame is clearly serious about this safety test then I need to quit my silly jokes and act my age. Anyway I'm tired, I just can't sleep well these days. Thankfully the weather is warm, there's hardly a hint of a breeze and as I have just four clients to look after, it shouldn't be too challenging.

Like she said, I'll just do what I normally do: get changed. The moment I slip off my trainers the office phone rings. There's a pause and then a young-sounding volunteer shouts for some help. No one else seems to be around so I make my way to help out the volunteer. Relieved, she hands over the phone, whispering: "No idea what they're saying."

Whoever it is has quite a strong Scottish accent, but seems clear enough. "I need to find Jack. Is he there?" he asks loudly.

"Not at the moment," I reply.

"Lass I've a mind to speak to him, what's he look like?"

Without thinking too deeply I draw a portrait for the caller as I walk back to the changing rooms so I can change my clothes. "Bald, but he'll be wearing a hat, shorts and in Palm paddling gear. He's tallish, about 5.10 and quite solid. Looks fit..." Just as I'm tying the laces on my left trainer I notice in the changing room mirror that there's someone staring at me.

"Sup-rised?" says Jack winking, clearly unable to resist teasing me. Then quieter he mouths, "Who wants to know?" before miming for me to put the phone on speaker. I shrug a yes and ask the caller who they are. "I've already told you, the caretaker at Islington Academy," comes a gruff voice.

"Not here," responds Jack, swiftly backing out of the women's changing rooms where he definitely shouldn't have been.

"I'm sorry but he's not here today. I'll leave a message you called, but I've got to go now too, there are clients waiting," I say in a rush to hit the red button. Note to self, never get involved in office calls again, and definitely never describe someone while they are listening, it's cringe making.

"I was using 'fit', the old school way," I mutter when I pass Jack on the way to the meet and greet with our first paddler to arrive, Kalani. Unfortunately Karen, Louise and the one whose name I'll never remember, but also begins with an L, rock up 10 minutes after their session should have started. We have this informal rule at #OutdoorSisters, the official name of Flame's stand-up paddleboarding business, that we wait for five and then go. But this doesn't work if practically every client turns up late. As a result of this muddle, I'm not entirely clear if the women know each other or know how to paddleboard.

Judging by Flame's tight smile, I guess she is thinking this is not a professional start.

Karen and Louise are in Sweaty Betty running gear and look the part. Kalani says she has just bought a Lidl board. Ms L seems stressed and is adamant that she needs to take her phone so she can take videos for her Instagram. I think she's some sort of influencer. I should just give her a waterproof camera case, but I'm trying to stop Karen walking into the Boat Club changing room as it's now full of Scouts (and that's a safeguarding no-no). Then I'm running to and from the big metal container where Flame keeps our boards and kit, surreptitiously trying to find the only XL buoyancy aid which will do up over Kalani's considerable bust without her thinking she's being swallowed by a boa constrictor. If only women designed buoyancy aids, or as Flame calls them, BAs.

"Welcome all to Hashtag Outdoor Sisters," says Flame warmly, somehow simultaneously giving me a daggers' look for totally failing to keep the calm, friendly vibe while kitting up. "We are so delighted you've come to paddle on the Regent's Canal, and we can't wait to share our water with you. Today I'm leaving you in the super capable hands of Lara. So have fun. And stay safe!"

Everyone looks at me. In the distance I can see Jack doing a sort of victory jig, Dad dance style, both thumbs up, arms raised above his head. This is when I should do an off-water safety briefing, but as if Jack's antics weren't distracting enough, just as I'm about to start with a safety talk that will relax the clients, and impress Flame, a Scout leader emerges looking for a lost Scout, closely trailed by 25 chattering Scouts. The noise is more than my Millennial clients, or Baby Boomer me, can cope with, so I point my hand towards the water and we head over to the pontoon. "Right so you all know how to do this?" I rush at them, "Jump on and paddle over to that narrowboat where we can discuss safety on the canal. If you don't know quite what to do, just copy me."

I should never have said 'jump'. Karen and Louise dare each other to leap, do it and both splash land. They flail around before grabbing the side of the pontoon and try, unsuccessfully, to pull themselves out. As the women haven't attached an ankle leash, their boards have now blown halfway across the basin – it almost looks as if Flame's fancy 10 foot sixes, Red branded, paddleboards are chasing Ms L who is the only one safely up on her feet and already paddling past the first moored narrowboat, presumably in pursuit of the perfect selfie. Poor Kalani is standing on the side looking almost shell-shocked. "I'm not sure I know how to jump on, as I haven't even blown up my Lidl board yet," she whispers, making me realise that I've also failed to pump up my own board properly. I try to stop panicking.

"Don't worry everyone," I say unconvincingly, but really just talking to Kalani, as the two water babies are clearly fine, even if they are dripping wet. "Let's start again! I think it's easiest if you climb out of the water up the rescue ladder and then sit on the wooden side of the canal with your feet on your board. Then put your leash on whichever ankle you prefer. When you're ready kneel on the board, facing to the front and then we can paddle after your friend. But before we have another go, I need a moment to just inflate my own board, looks like I didn't count the fleet quite right…"

I'm in my own little water world, SUP pumping like a pro, until the two wet women ask if it would be quicker to swim to their boards which are now mid basin. Maybe they should, I've got to get this session started.

Flame senses my confusion as she suddenly materialises on the pontoon with her own board and tells me that she'll just "retrieve the lost boards and your speedy client." She then paddles after the other woman who is barely in sight now that she's left the basin and got on to the canal, clearly a contender for the 11 Cities race. I must introduce her to Jack.

Eventually we're all together on the water and I have another go at that safety talk. It just comes out wrong.

"My last clients really struggled when we got to the death zone in Hackney – my little joke as a proud Islington postcoder – because that's when the wind picked up. So if you think you are going to crash into anything, like the paddler in front of you, boats or the side of the canal, just get to your knees."

"Oh whoops," yells Karen, falling into the canal for the second time, demonstrating exactly what I told the group not to do.

"Alright Karen?" shouts her friend. The head in the canal giggles happily.

"Yup, but how do I get back on the board? Is there a ladder here too?"

Wow this is getting complicated. I can't tell someone how to rescue themselves if I still haven't told the others how to paddle on the right side of the water, avoid sharing a tunnel or bridge underpass with a narrowboat and give space to all canal wildlife. Seeing my indecision, Flame paddles over to Karen to give her a quick heads up on how to self-rescue and soon she's climbing back on to her board. It really helps having an assistant.

I continue with my safety brief, just speaking a bit louder and faster. "And if you fall off just stay calm and try to swim back on to your paddleboard. Grab the handle and kick yourself on. Don't worry if it feels as if you've turned into a whale out of water, it looks much better than that."

"Like she said, Karen, you did look like a beached whale," says Kalani laughing as she replays her video of an inelegant heap scrabbling on to a paddleboard.

"I think I swallowed some canal water," says Karen looking a lot less happy, "does that matter?"

"No, it should be fine, just wash your hands and have a sniff of rum and cola, as that will kill off any bacteria," I reply quickly, because we've got to get going. I don't think this method is exactly an #OutdoorSisters recommendation. Flame can tell me later.

"OK ladies, let's get up on our boards, feet wide apart around the handle and then paddle." For a tranquil moment my clients organise their feet and start to paddle forwards. Ms L is not making any headway, if only I'd noticed she was facing the wrong way round then, easily done when you are as busy taking photos as her, but at that moment the swan family came around the corner.

Daddy swan starts hissing which seems to terrify this group – Karen panics, takes a step back and of course falls off, again, but at least this time I know she can get back on – while the others begin to shriek. One aims her paddle inexpertly at Daddy Swan.

I wish I could say I made this up, but someone on the towpath videoed it and sent it to our Boat Club (and all Instagram) captioned #*supshame paddlers hit swan* #*lovenaturehow*. Regrettably, I'm in the picture and Jack thought it all so hilarious he then shared it with the trustees, re-captioned, "No swans were hurt in the making of this".

Although that's not what it looks like.

Just when I think I've completely lost control of this little group, the wind picks up and is pushing us past the swan family, even Karen and her board are floating away from them, so the chaos comes to a quick halt. Flame reappears from nowhere, this time to help Karen wriggle back on to her board again. At the rate she's drinking the canal she's going to need to buy stocks in Coca-Cola.

"Can anyone park their boat here?" asks Kalani randomly.

I love it when the clients get interested in canal life and all the old warehouses now converted into fancy apartments. "Sort of, but they need to 'moor' not park – it's good to use the right boating lingo – and they need a licence from the Canal & River Trust. It's mostly shop and stop or 3-day stopovers," I begin to explain but Kalani has heard enough. She shouts towards the bearded guy on the big red narrowboat coming towards us "Yup, it's fine".

How did I not notice this massive boat?

Quick thinking time: I've got to avoid a clash between nine stone paddlers and a 20-tonne steel barge.

"Paddlers, let's get to the right side of the canal! No, it's the other side Kalani," I shout, rather obviously panicking. But it's not really Kalani who is having problems, it's Ms L who is stuck. In her head she was smiling to be #backonthewater while artfully positioned on a paddleboard with a towering old, London-brick chimney stack behind her, a post that would go viral. But in real life she's weeping as her board spins in the opposite direction to where she wants to go. What is wrong with her? Some people!

Thankfully the big boat chugs past and when I do a head count our little group are all on their boards, and have even coped with its tiny wash. What a relief.

Our mini journey gets us to the lock. Sometimes we portage around this, but today we've been going so slowly that it will make more sense to just turn around and paddle back to base. The others drop to their knees to munch the chocolate I've shared out, but Karen – twice dunked in the water and now super-confident, seems intent on exploring what yoga positions she can do on her board while watched by the people strolling along the towpath and a few who've set up ill-advised picnic spots along the lock wall.

"Well, I'm not a yoga specialist but I think you can do anything on a SUP board that you can do in the studio," I say enjoying being able to relax in the sunshine. Karen lies down, then tilts her tummy button to the sky and re-emerges as a crab in a backbend.

The people on the towpath, staring at us, start to clap, in a really nice way.

"The *ardha purvottanasana*," mutters Flame with the sort of frozen smile that suggests she's not impressed. That's weird as she's normally so excited by yoga. I take some photos.

Perhaps Flame guessed what would happen next… Karen, now the right way round, starts to feel dizzy.

We've got more clients turning up at 1pm, so we need to bring all our paddlers back to the Boat Club pronto. But with Karen dizzily incapacitated, the only answer is to tow her lying on her board until she feels well enough to paddle herself again. While I sort the towing out with lashings of knots, so the rope won't get away from either of us, she leans off the side of her board and is sick on to the front of mine, totally missing the canal. Oh yuck. If I ever see anyone being sick then I want to be sick, and… oh no… yep, here comes my own multicoloured yawn. Gross.

Fortunately Flame shepherds the three women in front of her, probably hoping that somehow, they'll miss the vomitorium. This gives Karen and me – both pale-faced – enough time to recover, slosh our boards clean of the sick with canal water and follow the leaders.

I paddle shamefacedly at the back, dragging Karen and her board, thinking about the impossibility of Flame giving me a happy sandwich of feedback seeing as most of the clients fell in, a swan was threatened, a boat nearly mashed us up and no doubt more…

*****

"Well at least no one got forgotten. Or died," says Flame tensely after the group has left while helping me to hose the last traces of vomit off the boards. "But it would have been good if you'd noticed the woman who was facing the wrong way round for half the journey; knew that inverted yoga positions are a risk without experience (and breakfast), and there's absolutely no way you should ever again tie one board to another. Just hand your client the rope and they can stand or kneel on it without risking rope burn. Never mind, as I said, it could have been more of a catastrophe. You might have driven off without saying sorry." She smiles with rather gritted teeth, eyes dull.

Oh no. Could she know about that cat already?

I smile back, nervously. "Thank you Flame. I've definitely got a lot to build on, especially my safety knowledge. Safety is just so important when you're working with water."

I've never felt so serious in my life. Thankfully Flame's yoga training seems to bless her with added tact, otherwise I'm sure she'd ask me more about the cat incident.

Later I ring my friend Adebola and recall the day, paddle stroke by paddle stroke. Adebola is a Flame fan as she's done some yoga with her. She's already wormed out of me how irritating Jack drove over a cat, and clearly feeling a bit mischievous tells me to fess up, so as to hopefully seem more honest than Jack in the battle for the business. I'm not keen, but then I say cunningly, "Only if you'll let me give you a paddleboarding lesson? You won't have to pay for a thing."

Adebola chortles, totally unoffended, because as she says, "That is never, ever going to happen. My Dad tried to teach me to drive in Nigeria – some sort of misplaced bonding – and my Lagos best friend took me out a few times too and it was hideous with them both. One shouted at me and the other just seemed disappointed. Friends and family are friends and family, not instructors."

"Well whatever you say I really can't talk about that cat with her, it's already given me full on PTSD," I snap just before the connection drops out. This often seems to happen with our calls, but Adebola's always been adept at moving on to the next thing.

"Was there something you didn't want to tell me?" says Flame unexpectedly passing with a bundle of paddles.

Caught out I put the full blame on Jack. Gratifyingly, Flame doesn't seem at all surprised.

4. OF MICE AND MEN

Boat Club life with Lara, Jack and Gladys

"I'd like to know why I've never been on a houseboat?" I say just to fill the silence at the Boat Club. It's the only thing related to water and the canal that my friend Adebola ever asks me about, so I need to find out more. She's definitely bored of me describing the Boat Club's boat which internally looks just like an office with its cables, computers and an electric kettle. It also sits rather low in the water so there are no windows to look out of. In her mind a canal boat should have billowing curtains and a kettle singing on top of a cosy woodburner stove, like life in *Simple Things,* plus swans floating past. She'd also like it to have an electric spa, for a bit of *Wallpaper** style, with an option to walk to a chic cocktail bar, fancy deli and a supermarket, none of which should be more than a 10 minute stroll away. I sort of think that too, although the nearby cafe on a converted barge where we sometimes go for a cuppa (to get away from the Boat Club kettle) is usually done up with more of an eye to artistic zing than canal charm.

Everything seems unnaturally quiet in the Boat Club paddle store without Capital FM blaring away. But our radio broke yesterday, when Jack banged the dials after hearing a 5-second news story about water pollution because it made him "feel like tearing his skin off and then vomiting."

"Well, I can answer your houseboat question Jack," said Gladys, rattling her cleaning cart on the way to the changing rooms. She seems to have mistaken my voice for his. "Your other job is as a rodent killer. All the narrowboats have mice. Why would you be invited on board if you then started nosing around cupboards or tried to force poison on to the people living there? No one would appreciate that."

"A rat catcher?!" I say startled. "Jack's job? I thought you worked here full time."

"Yeah that was your sup-osition," he says defensively while digging a screwdriver into the radio innards, which I'm guessing will be fixed soon. "I don't know many paddlers who survive just by paddle coach work, do you Lara? And 'pest control', as we say these days, fits well round the hours – it's Monday to Friday, nine to five, not weekends and evenings. Plus, it's a job that gives me a van," he says unnecessarily showing me a photo on his phone of a white Ford transit with the words "Call the Pied Piper for quick results" emblazoned on the side. "Best of all it's much busier in winter when it's not so fun on the water. Yes, evil laugh from me, the rodent control professional. Mice always come inside in December, it's their Christmas party instinct." He then mouths like a sulky child at Gladys' rattling back, "Anyway everywhere in Islington has got mice and plenty of people have rats too, it's not just narrowboats."

Too right Jack.

*****

I am trying to forget the scene with Greg last month. After we'd eaten a microwaved lasagne for supper he said, "I want a break." I laughed, and as I went to do the dishes said, quite seriously, "Me too, I was just thinking it would be fun to go to Milton Keynes and look at the canal there." I'd been wanting to try paddleboarding on the Grand Union for a while and thought maybe it could coincide with a pub lunch.

And then I looked away from the few suds it takes to wash up our two plates and I saw that Greg meant a break from me.

"It's India I want to go and see. And I want to see it on my own. You wouldn't even know how to enjoy a proper holiday. All you do at the weekend and in the evenings is go to that boring Boat Club. Yes, we were jogging along for a few years without the kids at home but ever since you got obsessed by paddles up, or whatever you call it, you've changed. Even your friends can't bear to be with you now."

For a second I feel real shame that I'd mentioned to him that Adebola was proving hard to meet as she always wanted to go out to dinner or drinks, and that's not affordable any more.

I let the half-clean plate slide back into the washing up bowl and with my hands still wet leant against the kitchen sink. I couldn't think of anything to say, except the word "India?".

"I'm catching a flight tomorrow to Chennai. It's at 19.50."

The room was so silent I could just hear my watch ticking, and it doesn't tick.

"Are you coming back?" I eventually tried to ask, not even sure what answer I wanted.

"I don't think so. I mean I'll come back from India when I'm ready, but not back here."

"Do the kids know about this?" I said eventually, starting to feel angry. How could he even afford to go to India? And how long would be enough? And what then?

"No, you can tell them what you want Lara. I've told you many times that they don't live here, and they're not kids anymore. They absolutely do not care what I'm doing or what you're doing. And you shouldn't care either. So I've told you my plans and now I'm going out for a farewell drink with Tim and my football gang, just to say goodbye." And then he walked out of the kitchen, not even kissing me goodbye. Seconds later he'd slipped on his jacket, leaving an empty peg, and was out the front door.

I sat in shock for no time, or hours, I'm not sure. I only got up to go to bed when the kitchen chair became too uncomfortable to stay put for longer. I was expecting Greg to come back for his bag, or to say "April Fool," not that he really did jokes, but he didn't.

It was an embarrassing end to 25 years of marriage, and not one I've shared with anyone yet. I hated myself for not being surprised by this surprise. I think love had fizzled out years ago. That first absent night I began wondering how to pay the mortgage without his salary. But real panic set in when I heard the scratches and rustling under the floorboards. Now I can only sleep with all the bedroom lights on.

*****

"How can you be so sure that all the houses have mice?" I push, thinking nervously about the scrabbles under my floorboard, the little black trails of hyphen droppings on the washing machine and breadboard. The sightings of what looks like a clockwork toy crossing to the skirting board, but when I spin round it's gone. The night invasions. It's definitely worse since Greg left. I wonder if he used to set traps?

"You live in one of those Victorian terraces Lara don't you?" asks Jack. I nod. "Figures," he says with a sort of snigger before explaining as if talking to a fool. "Well, those houses are all attached via floorboards, cellars and attics so the mice, clothes moths, rats, all the vermin, just scuttle between neighbours. Pests don't need a front door with a fancy knocker. Your terrace is their pest palace."

It's tempting to snap that, it's having this violent job that's made him so unphased by killing cats, because *they're the competition*. But maturely, I stay calm in a bid to get us all back on what should be relaxing houseboat chat. Luckily Gladys is close by again, this time sweeping. "Have you been on a houseboat Gladys?"

For a moment she raises her eyes skyward. It's as if she's got a real lot to say, but it's not right for me to hear today. "Oh yes, plenty times: cleaning, repairing, painting. But I'm too old now, the steps do my back and knees in."

I thought Gladys and I were friends, but just recently she's seemed more abrupt.

With an hour before the next SUP session I start to scroll through river and canal boats for sale and rent. It's amazing how people turn once filthy, working boats into a sanitised rectangle. They're expensive too, this one permanently moored at a wharf near us, *Poppy*, is renting out for £36,000 per year. I'm just wondering about how to fill it with furniture that mice won't like when ping, a WhatsUp from Flame arrives.

"Can you also run a sunset tour today? Sorry so last minute, but I've got this late booking from a group who r hoping for a red sky in their pix."

"Wow, I didn't even know you could paddle at night," I say out loud.

"It's not *night* Lara, it's a 'sunset' paddle so we'll be off the water before it's dark," explains Jack. It is so annoying that I'm always learning from him; my naivety is clearly encouraging him to mansplain.

"Wait a mo, how do you know what I'm talking about?" I ask, puzzled.

Jack picks up his phone and waves it at my face. "She sent it to me too."

He then switches the seemingly fixed radio on, jiggles the volume higher, and starts to sing along tunelessly. Now I know why Dizzy dresses in huge ear defenders.

5. AT THE *BUDDLEIA* NARROWBOAT CAFE

Lara and Gladys go for coffee

I've tempted hard-working Gladys to come out for a coffee with me. It took several invites but finally I succeed, by offering to do a mini photo shoot to celebrate her new hairdo. Gladys loves being photographed when she's had her hair done, but I think she's got bored of the Boat Club staff inevitably including the kayak shed with its rainbow display of boats in the background. This time I suggest we pop over to the *Buddleia* Narrowboat Cafe as it will easily provide fabulous backdrops for Gladys to strike a pose – teacups, fairy lights, crazy art, maybe even canal royalty.

Everyone on the canal knows the woman who runs this cafe (or needs to). The hitch is that Bio Queen is not always very friendly. I think a cafe should try and be nice to its clients, but Bio Queen, her outsize jewellery jangling, doesn't follow this old-fashioned rule. As for the food front, it's either delicious or the counter-top is bare. Mostly she stocks the *Buddleia* Narrowboat Cafe fridge with superstore-sourced croissants, zesting them up by serving them warm with a delicious dollop of homemade blackberry jam. Occasionally she'll just cook big spicy Moroccan stews filled with veggies gifted by one of her many contacts. She also always has tiny chaser-sized paper cups available to purchase for 50p which she then fills with healthy goose and duck food – frozen green peas. Just occasionally I swear that the paddleboarders are used as targets by the pea-pot purchasers, probably egged on by Bio Queen.

It's wrong to talk bad of canal royalty though.

Bio Queen's had a hand in setting up Islington's allotments, play groups, babysitting circles, OAP lunch clubs and a food bank, but besides canal life what she really loves is art – buying, selling, making, doing and artists. As a result, her cafe's tables are often crowded with clay figures and handmade ceramics being collected in readiness for sale, an enterprise that really picks up as we get closer to the date of the autumn Canal Festival. Today our heads are brushed by prayer flags, unearthed from one of her long-ago Nepali trips – she's a big climate activist and so definitely doesn't take plane flights these days. Her old narrowboat's wooden floorboards are covered with a couple of colourful rag rugs made a decade ago by a group who wanted to relearn the skills of a vintage canal tramper. Between two portholes are life-size paintings in mostly reds and greens of Bio Queen and a friend nude modelling – the result of a recent life class run on board. She's called one *Show STOPper*, the other *GO Go Girl* to stick with the traffic light colouring theme.

It's hard to keep up with Bio Queen's interests. Sometimes the Boat Club staff joke that the little cosy nook on board with its pink velvet cushion, and a direct view of the gang plank entry, is reserved for her ghost writer and the autobiography that will surely be a bestseller. Bio Queen hoots at this idea, instead calling it the chair-in-waiting for her next significant other. Meanwhile one of the arty visitors' dogs, and once an Indian runner duck which spent the day quacking orders, can often be found snoozing there.

Today, to support a Crowdfunder for the purchase of one of Bio Queen's recently deceased friend's wicker coffin, a couple in matching army fatigues are stripping willow and soaking it in the avocado-shaded, 1970s bathtub that is more usually used to keep cans of drinks icy cold.

"Well hello strangers," says Bio Queen marching up the gangplank with a basket of dandelion heads destined for a gastro transformation, interrupting my efforts to take portrait photos of Gladys. Today her smile is wide enough to swallow one of her famous croissants. "I've been wanting to see you both!"

Friendly Gladys leans over to give Bio Queen a hug. They've known each other for years. I wave cheerily and settle at a table with a view out of the boat on to the canal. I don't much like the boat's position as it's under a set of electric pylons that ping static into anyone with thick hair, but there's an impressive view of our yellow-painted Boat Club buildings from most of the starboard side; it's like being a spy.

Not that I've got much chance of practising the subtle art of seeing without being seen when with Gladys. Now the photo-taking is over she puts her hand out, clearly suggesting that she'd like to look through the images, so I pass over my phone hoping she'll find a couple of images she likes, while I focus on Bio Queen's chat.

"So, I hear everyone's in the running for the great business opportunity of the century!?" says Bio Queen, at least I think this is a question, but it turns out it's not. Bio Queen, who invariably has messy dyed red hair rolled up in a top knot, is today wearing a huge green sun-bleached velvet jacket that reeks of patchouli. She's adorned with a cluster of oversize necklaces that seem to add sparkle to her gossip as she leans over the table – one eye directly on the distant Boat Club – and starts to tell us what's been going on in the race for Flame's business.

"Not sure how much you want the job darling, but Jack's doing far better than you despite his many shortcomings," she says tilting her eyes at me coquettishly. "Flame told him he just had to stick to the canal, and he almost managed it. If he wasn't so loud she probably wouldn't have realised just how many liberties he takes crossing into the out of bound zones."

Curious, I ask when Jack's safety test was, but she waves my interruption away.

"And the Holly Pye friend is continuing her secret successes, not that some people will ever notice..." As ever, Bio Queen is confusing. I know it's rude, but I whisper in Gladys' ear to "just ignore her". But strangely Gladys has given up studying her photo show reel and seems as fascinated by me at Jack's exploits.

"Flame is giving everyone a test – well you both know that! She gave him a group of 10, and he took them into Wenlock Wharf. Someone bumped into a resident's boat, and someone else started taking photos of a washing line festooned with underwear. Hilarious! Eventually a group of residents lost it, and started to shout that Jack was illegally inside a wildlife sanctuary. They've been very antsy since that swan attack you engineered Lara..."

She breaks off for a moment to list, with some glee, the rather boring animals that have protection in the shallow, smelly waters of Wenlock Wharf – newts, dragonflies, damselflies, gnats, several yellow flowers, a pensioner terrapin and a ragged 'Stay In the EU' flag that's apparently a Green Flag-certified insect hotel. "Well you can imagine they were all in perilous danger with Jack's group," she trills, delightedly.

"Then Jack shouted back at the residents, to 'leave it out 'cos I've been paddling here since I was a kid'. He can be so annoying to intellectuals who live on boats: we could hear the shouting from here. Not clever of him, but he doesn't shy from conflict. Long story short, he skedaddled, but then managed to leave one of Flame's clients behind. In the panic no one had seen that she'd dropped her asthma inhaler and had to stop to try and fish it out. Luckily one of the nicest Wenlock Wharf residents saw she needed help, and in one of those strange canal twists invited her in for a coffee on their narrowboat. The start of a beautiful friendship I feel, but Jack didn't notice he'd lost that one. It's a small thing when you think about the world's umpteen problems, but Flame wasn't happy."

"That's very interesting," I say as if it wasn't improving my mood 100 per cent. I hadn't expected Jack-who-knows-it-all to make such big mistakes with clients. "Oh, it gets worse," continues Bio Queen with a happy smile. "He then leaps on to his motorbike in a tearing hurry and heads off down the towpath, which is definitely illegal, only to run into a cat that was just getting used to new moorings. The couple were so upset. We'd enjoyed watching them walking pussy on a lead but either it's too injured or too dead to do that now… "

"Dead?" say Gladys and I, equally shocked.

"That man's incorrigible. There's a nasty rumour that he also ran over the caretaker's cat by the academy in his fancy car a few days before and he hasn't apologised to anyone yet. Poor Scottish Bob – that's the school caretaker – is so upset. In fact, I don't suppose you'd like to make a donation towards the vet fees, we've also got a Crowdfunder for Snowdrop the Cat?" She looks pointedly at me, clearly knowing the something I'd rather she didn't.

"But if the cat is dead, why would there be vet fees?" I ask cautiously.

"Because Bob carried Snowdrop, who was actually a gift from his wife just a few weeks before she passed away, 10 years ago now, to Canonbury Vets and they charge for consultation, freezer storage and cremation in a little pet coffin. The bill was £4,000, about the same as my friend's wicker coffin will cost," she adds rattling bangles and necklaces rather like Scrooge in his ghostly chains. "Of course, you can always donate to that as well if you want, just log on to the Willa Wicker Crowdfunder."

"Yes, I'll definitely help," I gush, though I'm not sure if I've agreed to one or two donations – anything to stop her stream of consciousness, "but could me and Gladys just have a cuppa as we've both got to get back by half past." Bio Queen tuts and walks off.

She's back almost at once with croissants and hot drinks steaming from enamel mugs.

Gladys winks and pats me on the arm as she takes a bite of the warm croissant before saying, "No one knows about you and Bob's cat!" I smile relieved and then look at her in horror. "But, but..."

"I'm just joking," responds Gladys. "Why would you have anything to do with Jack's trail of destruction? When he was a teenager at the Boat Club, he's been coming to it for years you know, I remember him pulling a drowned fox out of the canal by its tail. I thought he was going to put it into the big council bins, but instead he slipped it into a black dustbin bag and left it in the club room. That was tidy, but it caused a terrible stink. It took quite a few months to get rid of the smell. In truth I've never liked Jack much since then. Though he did improve. And, of course, he's very good at paddlesports, like Ellie."

I smile back at her, as non-jealously as I can, then echo, "Yes, very good at paddlesports."

Even if Flame is deterred by blokey Jack's safety record, and she might not be if she reckons he can adapt his teaching style (and she can ignore his wanton lack of empathy with pets) I think Jack needs to pick up an injury if I want him ruled out of this business race. Let's hope his insane obsessions with endurance and racing will help with that.

It's weird how you can suddenly want something you didn't know you wanted only because it suddenly seems impossible to get. Or maybe I mean possible to get. I'm not sure.

"What do you know about Ellie then Gladys, is she another boat club regular?" I ask.

"Well, she's been Flame's friend for a long time. Are you sure you don't know her – you've got at least one photo of her and Flame on your paddleboarding shots?" replies Gladys gesturing at my camera. She'd clearly scrolled too far.

"Oh wow, you are so brilliant, could you just show it to me as I really don't think I'd ever recognise Ellie," I gush, curiously. Thank goodness for offering to photograph Gladys today. Mission one – get to know your competitors – is about to be ticked off.

"I think you would pick her out easily," continues Gladys shifting herself into a more comfy pose. "You see she's only got one leg. Look, it's this woman," she says pointing to that pic of Flame and the blonde woman doing yoga in the basin a few weeks back.

It's not like Gladys to be weird but there's definitely no one-legged woman on my phone's photo gallery nor at the Boat Club. I mean the disabled toilet and shower hasn't been used for months, years maybe.

So changing the subject, I ask her how her date went, but she just looks huffy. "I can dress up when I want you know, I do it for me, not just for a man!"

NOT THAT DEEP

Unbidden, Gladys has yet again given me a good life lesson.

6. SUNSET TOUR

Today's clients paddling with Lara and Jack: Ed, Lionel, Sarah, Natasha, Shiree

It's only when we're on the water – five clients keen to see the sunset after a day at their desks, plus me and Jack – that I realise I haven't said goodbye to Gladys. I give a cheery salute of my paddle in the boat club's general direction. Minutes later my phone buzzes.

"Just ignore it Captain Lara," says Jack as he overtakes a large hissing goose on a speedy touring board that is loaded with two dry bags full of useful kit including a first aid pack and a spare paddle. You'd think he was actually going somewhere more challenging than a 2.5 km paddle down our local canal to snap the sunset.

"You're on the water, chilling. Get yourself into that blue mind for a relaxing sup-erfix," he adds, clearly noticing that my mind's on the phone, not work. This is an unexpectedly good tip from Jack, especially as I'm not sure of the protocol when I'm with clients and my phone interrupts. Should I check and see if it's something important? Could we have left someone behind? Or is it maybe news of Greg in India? On balance I would probably ignore it, but just because Jack said that's what I should do, I counter intuit and take a peak.

"Lara r u K?" It's from Flame and she's still typing. "Gladys said u sent distress paddle signal to the Boat Club just now."

"LOL," I type soggily. "All OK."

"Yes, I thought u wouldn't know that signal, get Jack to show u asap. x"

Well, that's not going to happen Flame! And, thanks to responding to her message I'm now practically a sunrise behind the group. Fortunately, there's a steaming wind pushing the board forward, so it's not too much effort paddling.

"You're fast paddlers," I say rather out of breath to clients Ed and Lionel (identical looking, except for beard styles) when I finally catch up at the first lock – the one with the gorgeous flowers some guerrilla gardeners have taken over – which has a drop of 2.4 metres (eight feet in old money). Their three friends, all women working on web start-ups, and Jack have already carried their boards down the steep towpath slope to a place where we can easily get back on the water. As the guys and me pick up our boards and follow hurriedly down the towpath to get back on the lower water – sunset won't wait – we hear a commotion in front of us. Turns out there's a cyclist upturned in the canal. His two cyclist pals are crying with laughter. "Well done Freddie," they chortle. The poor bloke stands up, belly deep, then unclips his helmet to empty out the water, cartoon style.

"You OK mate?" says Jack kindly, manoeuvring his loaded paddleboard expertly to help the wet cyclist pull himself out on to the concrete side. The canal is so shallow by this edge that one of our paddlers, Ed, hops into the water to rescue the bike without even getting his buoyancy aid wet.

Everyone's talking at the cyclist who seems to think he was whacked into the canal – like wood on willow – by Sarah's board when the wind caught it. Sarah looks more mischievous than apologetic as she offers the cyclist a bit of homemade brownie. "Call it a 'peace offering'," she says, "but do you mind if we hurry on as I really want to get some photos of tonight's sunset…"

That's nice I think, a bit of sugar for the shock.

Natasha, also paddling with us, has had time to get a phone number from one of the cyclist's bankside laughing friends. It's Shiree who stops us from delaying any longer by impatiently slapping at her arms and ankles. "Bees up by the lock and now there are horrible biting insects everywhere," she grimaces, "Gnat nice. We've got to outrun them."

Lionel, overhearing, pulls a mosquito hood out of his pocket and places it over his head. "That must be expedition wear with plenty of stories to tell," says Jack at his most friendly. "Nah," laughs Natasha, "he's just weird about winged things getting stuck in his waxed tash. Doubt he'll see the sunset wearing that net!"

We all push off. At the next bridge, with yellow graffiti needlessly reminding us that 'it's getting hotter', I get distracted by high pitched beeps, look up sharply and then end up bumping Jack's narrow board. He lurches, but manages to stay glued on. Unfortunately, his board shoots forward into Natasha's and the surprise attack sees her unbalance to splash land into the canal. Shiree and Lionel both try to paddle towards her, presumably to encourage her back on, when suddenly they start jabbering at each other, ducking as if pellets are being hurled at them. Lionel raises a paddle and beats at the air above their heads.

I can't see what the problem is but someone else has, and they're filming us which Natasha, who is facing the bridge and still in the water, seems to be really agitated about. So cross that she won't climb back on to her paddleboard. If only I'd not been too proud to ask Jack how to do that distress signal because I need his help now.

Looking up I can see that there are about 15 dark shadows above us, using the old arched bridge to bat watch, although now they're also observing dramatic human interaction with bats. The group is using a little black detector box that picks up the high-pitched bat squeaks as they flit past on their early evening gnat-feast, which I guess is what distracted me in the first place. At least I hope the sonic screams are a decoy, or even real bat feeding noise, not a terrified I'm-a-bat-about-to-be-hit noise. Now I've figured out what's happening, it's cool seeing the silhouette of fast flying bats wheel around the old bridge as they hunt insects for dinner. I'd heard that Regent's Canal was big on bats, and for some people this is exciting news, but clearly our insect-wary group do not like them at all.

"What if they get tangled in my hair?" shouts Lionel swiping wildly. He seems to have forgotten that he's wearing a hair net and unaware that he's turned from a 30-something six foot adult into a traumatised eight-year-old. Meanwhile, Shiree has either been hit by Lionel, or swallowed a bat, as she's now kneeling on her board grasping at her throat as if she can't breathe.

"Panic attack," says Jack pointing at Shiree. "Lara, can you calm her down while I get the other woman out of the water?"

I'm not sure I can manage either task, but fortunately Shiree responds well to me patting her arm and slowly gets her breath back under control. I've never seen a panic attack before, but thank my lucky stars that CPR wasn't needed. Jack's busy too. He waves his paddles at me and then waggles both of his arms up and down as if he was doing some warm up for a circus act. I ignore him.

Jack blows a whistle.

Again, I ignore him. Well, I'm dealing with Shiree.

One of the silhouettes on the bridge throws a doughnut down at me, like they're feeding the bears at the zoo. If that's what you're allowed to feed bears these days. If bears even are in zoos. "Oi, watch it," I say hungrily as the bun has ended up in the water, so no good to anyone. "You need to help your mate with that girl over there. We're calling 999," someone shouts from the bridge parapet.

Now I'm in panic mode. I can hear a high-pitched whine, I think it's me, shouting "Oh my God," over and over. It's so annoying that no wonder Lionel stops his crazed bat attack and accidentally drops his paddle across my back. It really hurts, but brings me back to my duties. I take a breath and ask what's left of our little group to paddle towards the side of the canal so we can sort ourselves out. And a good thing I managed this, because at that moment a narrowboat noses through the tunnel towards Natasha's limp body.

We all shout at the boat driver who tries to switch into reverse and ends up banging the brick arch with such a jolt that the bat watching group above must assume there's been an earthquake.

And then, just like that, everything is calm again. Natasha chokes back into consciousness thanks to Jack's efforts, and the narrowboat putters past with a friendly wave. Very soon a siren blasting ambulance arrives and we encourage Natasha to get checked out by leaving her in a damp pile on the towpath with the medics.

I look at my watch and notice we haven't even been on the water for 40 minutes.

Sarah dishes out more bits of 'naughty brownie', as she calls it, for the shock. I take three and very quickly feel light-headed, so I'm glad that it's time to turn back even if that means now paddling into an ever-strengthening wind. It's getting proper dark by now. Even if it felt as if time stopped during the bridge and bat furore, the sun seems to have set, which means our group managed to miss taking any red sky photos. Their post paddle feedback has no hope of being 5 star. Oops.

Just by Eagle Wharf's handsome old brick chimney the wind drops and our canal is beautiful again, lit up by a glimmering surface dotted with the lights from the towpath apartments. Suddenly the breeze rolls back, ruffling the water surface so that all the reflected lights seem to be bouncing along the canal like lost ping pong balls.

I'd like to tell Flame what's happened, so she doesn't worry if we're back in the boat yard a bit late. I drop to my knees and tuck my board into the side, out of the wind, to WhatsUp her. When I look up again, I can hear creaking wings and then see the dark shape of three summer-solid Canada geese flying along the canal towards our paddlers. I'm guessing the noisier two at the front are complaining about being chased out of the territory by the almost pantomime aggressive honking goose at the back. Their wings creak and swish in unison as the absorbed goose trio, pushed along by the wind, hog the waterway until they meet our paddlers. Although the first goose manages to veer successfully past Sarah, who is now at the front, the other geese can't gently brake or dodge the next three people paddling in a row, with not a light between them, so fly beak-first into the torso of Lionel, then Shiree and finally Jack. Ouch.

All three have been hit by a goose.

Everyone is in the water.

"Help!" I shout weakly, although I'm completely fine. I press wildly at my phone managing to accidentally record live the full goose attack aftermath for Flame as a WhatsUp voice note. She never does tell me what she made of my inept ability to rescue anyone, perhaps because she spent the next morning thanking everyone in the bat group who fortunately came to the rescue of her paddlers, again.

SPLASH "What the f**"
"Are they dead?"
"Get me out of here." SPLASH
"Where's my paddle?" SPLASH
SPLASH "It's in my hair, get it out!"
"It's OK everyone, just a goose near miss." That's Jack.
"Direct hit more like."
"Did we hurt them?"
"I can tell you that I feel hurt, bloody birds"
Hysterical laughter. That's me…

I reckon the bat fans heard the furore as paddlers and birds simultaneously tipped into the canal, all equally shocked by what hit them. Anyway they sped towards us to see who needed rescuing. By this time the poor birds had given their pale belly feathers a shake, honked bitter warnings to each other and paddled off into the dark, territorial argument forgotten, leaving three people in the water, bruised rather than bloodied. Even Jack, who suffered a low strike, needs encouragement to clamber back on to his paddleboard. Eventually our party is ready to try for home again.

"Something like this could only happen to you." (Sarah to Lionel)
"It is no laughing matter."
"Goose attack thwarted!"
"Those birds must be six kilos or more."
"Wonder how they feel then, I'm 12 stone." That's Jack (the animal lover!).

"Try saying honk when you see the next gaggle of geese."

Hysterical laughter. That's me, again...

As we paddle the last stretch back to the Boat Club a waxing moon rises to the east, but hanging so low it is dwarfed by the 24-floor and higher tower blocks fencing the City Road from the basin. Suddenly, everyone but me falls quiet, worn out by the unexpected adventure of this after work paddle.

I just can't stop giggling. Those geese! You'd have to see it to believe it really.

*****

"It was a proper nature battle tonight – gnats, bats and geese against us hardy paddleboarders, and 'did they give us one hell of a beating'! I never knew that animals hated people so much... Or maybe it was just that everything was out to mess up Lionel's hipster moustache, circa 2012?" I say jokily to Jack when we finally tidy up at the inky dark Boat Club base and our risk assessment breaking group have gone. I can't really concentrate, so I've failed to count our group's paddles away, or even everyone out of the yard safely. I do manage to ask someone to let us know how they feel tomorrow, especially Natasha.

"Yup, if we tell people all the things that happened tonight, no one is ever going to believe us," says Jack slowly, wincing from the misery of a goose-struck groin. "And please let me write the accident report as you were away with the fairies half the trip. I'll sup-erimpose it so it makes sense."

My giggles turn into hiccups. What is wrong with me?

It's so dark in the yard that I can't see Jack's expression. But much to my surprise I trip on a stray neoprene bootie and rather lurch into his arms. "One weed brownie and you're anyone's," he says sadly.

To be fair, I did eat three.

Whatever happened next − and I think he drives me home at his usual breakneck speed, managing to leave me safely on the doorstep of my mouse-infested, husbandless house − I now realise it would be foolish of me to keep pretending to hate him.

Jack is someone a person in trouble on the water can trust to save them, a sort of SUP-erman. Whereas me, I just turn into a silly giggling goose.

.

7. HEN PARTY

*Today's clients paddling with Lara and Jack:
Teegan, brother Zennor, and the girls*

Mostly Flame is super organised, and the SUP coaches (like me and Jack) just follow her schedule, adding ourselves into her spreadsheet to suit our convenience. But, increasingly there's a WhatsUp from Flame offering an emergency paddle opportunity. Today it's intriguing: "Sorry for late notice but could you do a hen party about noon today? With Jack? The girls have to finish at 2pm prompt so they can get to King's Cross for a rock n' roll makeover. 10 booked."

I'll say yes – working with Jack in the daylight will be a way for him to see that I'm just as capable as him when the circumstances are right, which he might feedback to Flame. What's more I'll be out of my lonely house, being paid to be on the water on a beautiful summer day. I'm sure Gladys would approve, except she doesn't seem to be obviously around today – although in the distance I do spot Dizzy getting a bucket and mop out of the cleaners' cupboard.

I find Jack already tinkering with a boat when I arrive at the Boat Club. "Look at these rowlocks," he says crudely when he notices there's someone lingering by the workshop. "Oh it's you Lara. How's your cat tally?"

"I'm not sure why you're asking me that?" I say, surprised by his attack, adding a bit huffily, "I'm not going to mention the geese, but a little bird says that you squashed someone's pet on the towpath as well."

"Ha, I see what you did there with the fowl – goose/bird – you'll get better at puns if you practise," laughs Jack good natured again. "Yup, that was awful. Cat was on a lead, not that I saw it, and then it must have taken fright at a dog walker and bolted right in front of my new MTB, That stands for mountain bike by the way. I went flying on to the gravel. I think I was a bit concussed, my crasher shell was totally trashed, look it's here," he says, gaining my sympathies as he picks up the dented red cycle helmet lying on the workshop bench. "I've been meaning to go round and take the couple some flowers from the Co-op as a bit of a sorry, but it's so busy here I haven't had a chance. Maybe you could do it for me?" he asks hopefully.

"There's no way I'm getting embroiled," I huff crossly. "I'm guessing the people whose cat it was are going to be really upset with you if they haven't moved their boat?"

"I sup-pose you're right, I was sort of convinced by Gladys to get the flowers, but she's busy today planning a BBQ so I can pretend I forgot," says Jack looking at the massive tracker gadget on his wrist in a bit of a panic. Actually we've got 25 minutes until the session starts. Plenty of time as the boards are already out.

"Does Gladys need some help cooking?" I ask but annoyingly Jack is back inside the workshop buzzing drills, so probably doesn't hear. He definitely doesn't answer.

She's easy to find thanks to the smoke billowing from the half barrel BBQ placed at the far end of the yard. As I go and inspect it's clear Gladys is in total control. She's set up a portable picnic table which looks like a butcher's stall, well a very high class one as most of the meat is in marinades. There's a smaller table laid out similarly, but with fish.

"Can you just scale these fish," she asks me pointing her knife at a row. I look blank. "Um, I'm not sure I know how to do that. Why don't you just buy fish ready to eat?"

"Sorry Lara, I thought you were my daughter creeping up. You Londoners never know nothing about scaling fish. When I first found this out it made me laugh so much given that your home is an island too," says Gladys laughing. "Now let's give you a lesson. Hold the fish by the tail. Scrape the knife towards the head and see how fast the scales fall away," as she demonstrates a cloud of contact lenses, presumably fish scales, are messily dislodged. I try not to let her see me gag.

"Mami, you get back to the flames, I'll handle the fish," interrupts Dizzy, adding for my benefit, "Sorry Lara, that's definitely not on your job description! I got a great price at Chapel Street market earlier with these bad boys, so it seemed like a good opportunity for Mami to do a cook-up for us all." She suddenly looks at me suspiciously and asks, "Do you eat meat?"

I'm not sure if fish cake counts, but I'm willing to give whatever her Mami is cooking a go.

Gladys and Dizzy seem pleased by my answer. Gladys adding, "Then at least you're not like that Jack, refusing the food the good Lord provided for us today."

"But Jack eats everything surely. Not to offend, but I think of him as greedy," I say thoughtlessly. Both Dizzy and Gladys tut. There's clearly bad blood about BBQs in the Boat Yard.

"I like corn on the cob and smoky peppers as much as anyone, but Jack has rules, he won't eat anything with a face. Or vegetables unless they are battered. What kind of a man is that?" asks Gladys resplendent in a white blouse protected by an oversize blue and white striped apron.

I give a sort of squeak as my synapses figure out what this means – the rodent exterminator is a vegetarian. But it's Jack who seems the most angry. "You're as bad as the rest of them Lara if you're judging me about not eating meat. I told you I don't like cruelty to animals and with my work watching the way even rodents have families and friends; build homes and groom each other, well there was no way I could then knowingly eat meat."

"He's been like this for years," says Gladys, "won't eat faces, even if I cut the faces off."

I know it's disloyal, as I do think Jack has the moral high ground here, but when he stalks back to the workshop I take two spicy chicken wings and one whole fish and wolf them down with bread and salad. Gladys nods her approval, promising that she'll save a Tupperware of BBQ treats for me in the project room if she's packed up by the time our hen party is back at the base.

Brilliant, that's my meal plans sorted out for the next week.

*****

Hen parties are a neat way to bring in cash and fill the diary with future bookings. They are usually high energy too. I'm certain Jack will be pushed off – not that he'll mind, plus it's pretty warm today and he's already dressed in his favourite blue Palm neoprene shorts. I imagine high spirits on the boards – Jack repeatedly dunked – while I sweep around supporting the nervous clients. What's not so great is that if this happens then Jack will take control of the session, leaving me looking like his assistant when we should be equal.

When we meet our hen party it's clear the girls don't need teaching any basics, though Jack can't resist a little mansplaining, but he is a paddlesports coach, so I suppose that's fair enough. Maybe I should write something to counter hectoring male voices in my business plan? That would be a good move for an #OutdoorSisters contender.

The group are mostly surfer chicks who spend their downtime in Cornwall or Portugal. They are henning it up in London for a spontaneous culture weekend as the weather report was for record breaking flat, no swell at all. They've just finished a bottomless brunch on Upper Street making the Boat Club smell faintly of mimosa. Thankfully chief bridesmaid Teegan says the girls – and her brother Zennor – are happy to wear buoyancy aids (a surfer novelty) and just chill. No one wants to wear shoes when they see Jack padding around the yard in his bare feet (not allowed!), so we have no choice but to break the rules and set out for the gentlest, flattest paddle the girls (and Zennor) have ever done. Right after the Bridge of Sighs by the pub (Jack's romantic name for the brick road bridge that crosses the canal) the group lose their wobbly alcohol stance and start to show off.

I take out my phone and video two headstands, a jousting match, three of the party hijacking the bride's board and Teegan cartwheeling into the water. Somehow, we gather the group into the side when a narrowboat comes through and then their antics begin again – mixing playfighting with a high-spirited chase across the boards. This group has no problem with being wet at all, it's a revelation after months of clients panicking at the thought of falling in, even when they're effectively glued on to their board by their knees.

"Come on Jack, Lara, join us!" shout the girls paddling over the next time there's a lull in their water play.

"It's OK, I'll just take some snaps of you all," I say, grateful for the photographic excuse.

But Jack is all for it and quickly absorbed in a makeshift British Bulldog game that lets the paddlers chase, clash and fall around the Bridge of Sighs, entertaining the lunchtime drinkers on both the pub's balconies overlooking the canal. After 10 minutes and two or three raucous immersions, Jack calls for time out, leaving the bridal party to it, and paddles back to me where he drones on about his personal trainer (or as he puts it "PT"). He says his PT (unnamed, no gender used even though he told me it was Ellie not so long ago) has given him a high protein, low fat, high intensity, low enjoyment (I made that up) programme "for every day of the week with a Y in it". He's smitten – but perhaps more with getting fit than with Ellie, it's hard to tell.

"What's so special about this PT you're working with?" I ask wheedlingly.

It's definitely a question he wants to answer in full. And as we're both stuck on paddleboards until Cornwall beats Portugal, or vice versa, I might even also learn how to get fitter and figure out more about Ellie's chances of being the new Flame. Surely as Jack's PT she's in a better position than him to run #OutdoorSisters? But he's also at the Boat Club most days so a safe pair of hands, with lots of Paddle UK CPD points and all sorts of qualifications as a coach and leader, whatever that means. It doesn't help that Jack has a habit of using abbreviations that leave me plain confused. If I ask what they mean he just smirks and says, "If you know, you know."

Pretending to take some more photos of our hen party I make a note on my phone to look up PSRC, CPD and

FITT. PT I've at least nailed. I can't imagine ever being as fit as Jack and still wanting to spend money on exercise. He's practically Olympic level in everything he does. But Jack seems to think that's when you should be spending...

"Your own PT makes a big difference. My PT sets such great goals. I really feel I'm on to something," he says enthusiastically. "Someone like me can write a fitness programme but I wasn't including the right ratio of strength to flexibility. They've got this idea that we stick to the FITT principle for all my workouts so I'm in control – choosing the FITT (that's the frequency, intensity, time and type of workout, Lara) depending on my mood and how my body feels after intense paddlesports. Yes, she sup-ervises, but it's a real partnership that I'm expecting will bulk me up, get me fitter and nail the racing," drones Jack moving fluidly from a central cross-legged position on his board into a nifty stretch that I suspect might be a clever move taught by the PT rather than fumbling to avoid pins and needles. Feeling stiff I try to copy his moves, only to wobble my board alarmingly.

"And they've got such good contacts. So, if I can bulk up on the shoulders and raise my abs too, then I reckon you'll be seeing me as a sup-erstar on the TV ASAP!" he continues.

At the Boat Club, paddling on TV is everyone's secret goal, inspired last year by Flame being spotted by a media company scout on their lunch break from an office nearby at Old Street. The media scout then calculated that a filming session on the canal on a sunny day was going to cut his budget, being so much cheaper than flying technicians, cameras, wardrobe and make-up to Croatia. A week later Flame did a few yoga poses and a couple of laughs to camera while bathed in rigged-up lighting. To our surprise the clip was then on TV within two months, with Flame looking as if she'd been transported to a swanky Mediterranean tourist resort with 38C sunshine. It's slightly embarrassing to Flame that the club was paid in metres of pastel bunting while she got cash, but in fact her moment of paddling glory inspired everyone at the Boat Club. Now Jack and the others, perhaps even me, are convinced that we will one day get our 15 seconds of fame with the canal as the perfect backdrop.

I'm not sure how to say this delicately to Jack, but after Gladys's big reveal earlier this week about Ellie I'm a bit confused – doesn't she just have one leg and maybe a bionic foot? But when I ask him cautiously, "Is Ellie fit enough to be a PT?" Jack just laughs. "She's so fit. An inspiration. And so balanced, I thought I was pretty OK at paddling, I mean I've always found it easy, but she can do more on one leg on these boards than I can do on two! She's almost as good as…" But he never finishes the sentence as we are interrupted by our hens' makeover schedule.

Catching the way Jack holds a pose when he's passing a narrowboat window, or randomly picks up his phone to check how he looks, it's clear his body looking beautiful is important to him. So, it's extra sad for Jack that when we bring our barefoot hen party back to the Boat Club he's the only one who manages to step off his board directly on to a rogue nail. I hear him swear, but then he plays it cool in front of our hens, simply leaving a line of bloody footprints like the *Little Mermaid*, if she ever had to hobble between our pontoon and the changing rooms.

"I'm not sup-erstitious but I may be gone for some time ladies!" he announces bravely as he pushes the injured foot into a big boot and heads off on his motorbike (latest new toy) towards the nearest A&E. At least I hope that's where he's going.

What the geese couldn't do, these hens have managed.

I idly wonder what doctors' orders are when it comes to mixing deep puncture wounds with polluted canal water, before realising this is my chance to get some more paddleboarding skills without Jack observing. What I need is a PT – wow, I never thought I'd even think that – or perhaps better, an intense course on some really clean water, a long way from this canal. By the time Jack is back on the water, I need to have upgraded my paddle skills. Surely it can't be that hard?

8. COACH CRUSH

Lara tries to skill-up, overseen by trainer Nigel and the guys on the course, Wilf and Rick

The trauma of last week's goose attack is gone. On the water today I felt like I'd turned into a super paddler – the sort I normally stare at on social media, puzzling how anyone can do such tricks. In my mind I moved effortlessly from warrior stance, back straight, eyes wide open and then into an elegant bounce which saw me spinning the tail end of my board. Round and round I pivoted anti-clockwise until I dizzily fell off into this beautiful, clean lake in Surrey. And struggle to get back on again.

"I think the board is just too new and clean," I say loudly after a third attempt to drag myself back up and on. Two of the guys on the course suddenly appear. One pins my board into a slope and the other shouts out "Remember this technique, wings and thighs," while hoicking me back on to my slippery board by lifting me up simultaneously under my right arm and left leg, as if I'm a slab of meat.

"Well done, good rescue guys," says Nigel the trainer who, like the rest of the group has a top torso so muscled his profile looks like a croissant. All winter this over-competitive man of the water surfs storm sea waves and kayaks white water rivers. All summer he's outside running this watersports centre, organising staff and club members, serving barista-good coffee and flogging last year's equipment to ensure he has the best for next season.

Nigel knows everything, and the other course participants will soon.

But I'm not having much fun. The wings and thighs manoeuvre might have got me back on the board, but I can barely look at my rescuers (aka the abattoir guys, Wilf and Rick who have their own watersports centres in Berkshire and Cumbria, respectively). The hair on the back of my neck is prickling with shame, and I feel a bit bruised. Although I'd struck lucky to find a refresher instructor course which let me tag along for a full day's practice, it turns out that I'm the only woman and clearly have been allocated the role of group pet. Right now I feel like a knocked-about guinea pig. The ones you eat.

I know you've got to learn and practice, that's why I borrowed a drysuit, but the brute strength of the five guys on the course, and Nigel's straight-talking feedback, is sapping my paddling powers. For the rest of the morning every time I try a new manoeuvre, I'm now up against fear of public shaming and sensible anxiety about whether I'll be able to skip, hop and jump forward (and backwards ffs) on my borrowed board in the same way that Nigel has just demonstrated.

I do wish he'd demo on land so we could have a go without any risk of a cold bath, but that doesn't seem to be an option for the guys. They just want to try it out and laugh at the losers who fall in. Is this why people go to a PT, for a bit of tailored sympathy rather than risk group shaming?

The training does start to help me though. Best bit of the day was nailing the cross bow turn and trying out a paddle on the very speediest and thinnest of boards. Now I can boast to Jack – and Flame – that I've been on a long hard board and managed a 100m burst on the holy grail of paddleboarding, a 14-foot race Starboard sprint with its wave-slicing, pointy nose. Nigel said the trick is to get your legs as wide as possible on the super-skinny 20-inch seemingly grip-free deck, bend your knees, relax unwanted toe gripping and then paddle furiously. The Starboard isn't very forgiving, but wow does it power along. With Nigel's encouragement (he's really talking to the guys) I'm almost inspired to enter elite races like Jack's 11 Cities, or would be if the distance was nine cities shorter. Turns out that I can: the choice for SUP racing varies from 100m to a perhaps even do-able 8km.

Hang on, that means paddling more than half of the Regent's Canal, without a snack stop.

It may be the end of July, with a nice 19C water temperature, but being in and out of the lake all morning is making me cold. By our lunch break I'm definitely exhausted. Lifting the 14 foot hardboard out of the lake gets dangerously close to putting my back out. Even guzzling two big slabs of sugary flapjack, bought at the cafe, doesn't re-fire my energy. The other course participants don't seem to be suffering at all. After topping up their water bottles they sit around gossiping about their SUP adventures.

One of the older guys – about 38 so not exactly 'old' old in the way that I'm old – knows the Boat Club and asks me for updates. "Is Jack still acting like the manager? What's the green weed situation, does the canal still look like a lawn in the summer?" I was zoning out until he suddenly asked, "How's One-leg Ellie getting along?" Turns out he knew Ellie back when she was a Boat Club youth member. "She's such a talented lady. And has amazing power and balance. I know you shouldn't really mention people's physical challenges, but I knew her as a teenager before her accident and she was good then. But now, with all her college training and hard work she's unique – a real inspiration for everyone. How do you get on with her, Zara? Has she taught you her one-leg pivot yet? It's fiendishly hard."

"It's Lara," I say crossly, thinking how the moon is more likely to crash into this lake than for me to even attempt a one-legged pivot.

"Well, to tell the truth, I don't know her very well," I admit.

"You do paddle a bit differently, but she's such a force of nature," he says thoughtfully. I seize the chance to be absolutely certain what Ellie looks like by asking him to show me a photo. He goes online and in seconds there are a million images of Ellie Senkruraj up on the net – with paddles, medals, influencer portraits and in head-spinning SUP yoga poses. It's definitely the woman in the photo on my phone, paddling with Flame and clearly on two legs. "But why do you say she's disabled?" I ask, puzzling.

"Well she had a bad kayak accident, so I guess not disabled. You can look up the detail and recommendations in the Marine Accident & Investigation Report," Nigel interrupts, obviously impatient to finish the training on time. "That's a useful resource for all of you, helps us all avoid the near misses. Now go order yourself another cuppa or top up and in quarter of an hour we can analyse the videos I shot this morning."

For the rest of the lunch break I flop on the lake's grassy bank, baseball hat shading my eyes, wondering how I've missed noticing Ellie. Revived by flapjack and tea the other SUP coaches get animated about why everyone should have a go at SUP racing.

They seem so keen that even I should try a race soon, that I begin to wonder if they don't get many entrants.

I don't like the sound of how you have to be a gadget whizz and submit a pre-race time so that you can be slotted into the right division. This is done over 2 km with Div 1 for the swifties who can get round in under 13 minutes. SUP slow isn't really that far off SUP fast as the snail group, Div 5, is for anyone who can paddle 2 km in over 18 minutes. Back at the Boat Club we can take 90 minutes just to get to the first lock. The timing gets technical because these guys seem to be digital natives *and* SUP experts, but apparently it's to stop people cheating. Turns out the verification has to be with a paddle-logging phone app, and before the actual race day, you need to decide if you want to do a technical paddle, executing multiple turns at speed, or a less likely to fall off contest around marker buoys (perhaps better for winter). At my age I'm a veteran, despite never having done a race in my life, although any age (including fast 50–60-year-olds) can enter the Open, which is also the section 18–29-year-olds compete in.

With so few people doing SUP racing or SUP endurance, and even less older women, could this be my next ambition? Who wants to pootle along the same bit of Regent's Canal getting cold waiting for jelly-legged clients intent on photographing the crumbling foundry chimneys, weak sunset or a duck-weed stained swan passing another narrowboat, when they could be pushing the sound barrier, with the aid of a PT on their phone's speaker, training for the Ice Breaker Series? My rival Jack, that's who, although with his wounded foot it's going to be more challenging for him.

But even if I upgrade my board, paddle and body, I'm not going to match Jack's ambition. Or Flame's experience. Or Ellie's PT knowledge. Or the guys on this course with their speed and power.

Actually this improvers' paddleboard course has been a major reality check, especially combined with flashbacks from that sunset debacle with gnats, bats and swans. Coach Nigel uses video to help clients sweat the small moves until they can effortlessly do 360 degree spins, but watching the videoed workouts I can see that though I'm doing the moves (that felt great), that person on the board (me!) looks terrible. Even standing, I stoop. I paddle rigidly in the same pattern. When I gather the courage to move a leg forwards a fraction, or back a demi fraction, my body turns into an old lady worrying about slipping on ice – not a good look for a SUP coach. I shamefully tag along at the back in the mock races, demonstrating a clear lack of competitiveness. On his video you can see me shift into lower and lower (metaphorical) gears as if to get a better look at a Canada goose, of which there are a large number on the lake, in the world, actually, (190,000 says Wiki). No one needs to be distracted this much by a bird unless they are especially interested in goose scatology, or not born to race.

Watching the videos with my re-trained, SUP-improver eye I can see that the guys really have mastered the moves. They may make the odd slip, sometimes falling, but basically their step-back turns rock. It is a shame that Nigel has lent me a high vis orange drysuit, ideal for avoiding power boats in the North Sea, while the others opted for their own sleek wetsuits, so wobbly me, whether messing up the race drafting exercise by failing to keep a trio of us paddling like pros or switching the trim, stands out – very orange, often shifting to my knees – in every vid.

The embarrassment gives me an attack of the giggles which, suppressed, turn into hiccups. Everyone looks at me in faint disbelief. Why is my body letting me down inside and out?

The guys are kind-hearted though about my orange convict-gear. "You'll get a good rest when they catch up with you," jokes Wilf. He clearly also thinks that I'm wearing a prison issue boiler suit.

Today's last session is a two-hour tour with rescue practice. Nigel offers me a carbon paddle which weighs less than the flapjacks I ate for lunch. He then points me towards a solid 10.6 Red board, just like I'm used to paddling on the canal, murmurs a few words of encouragement and off I follow, just like the others – all of us suddenly ducklings following Papa Nigel – to circle the lake in between practice rescues.

Just past the lake's little islands the hiccups come back again and nothing seems to make them stop. I abandon the plan (or rather adopt my plan B) in a bid to shake them. I take deep breaths. I drink half my water. I try and think about when I last saw a kingfisher in real life and not a *Countryfile* calendar. I lie flat on my back, which is a bit awkward when you're wearing a buoyancy aid. But still the hiccups come.

I only notice that the group has already done one complete circuit, and is now lapping the lake again when Nigel nudges my leg with his top-of-the-range carbon fibre paddle. I'm lying still on the board at this stage, so this attention is presumably to check I'm alive, although the hiccups are a giveaway. "Up you get, just go gently and you'll be fine, you can cut it short if you circle past the buoy and head to the pontoon for your rescues. We'll meet you there," he says kindly.

I intend to do what I've been told, when suddenly I feel like the flapjack's sugar overload has caught up with me. Wobbling on to my knees I see spots pulse in front of my eyes as if I'm caught in a lightshow: ah I get it, I'm overheating! As I'm encased in a drysuit the only way to cool down is to slither off my board into the water. But Houston we now have another problem: that cooling slap of water is doing strange things to my paddle-exhausted body and now I'm desperate to wee. This is solvable surely? I'm sure I can wee illicitly, there under water without anyone realising, so I go ahead, but then – double horror – I feel my right leg in its comfy leggings go strangely soggily wet as gradually the wee edges its way down to my all-in-one booties flowing from heel to toe.

I'd thought the rescue flips would be challenging, but now I'm determined to get off the water asap, just in case anyone figures out my rookie wee error. Sloshing around in a drysuit while I'm being 'rescued' would be beyond humiliating.

I'd have to change my name, SIM card, paddling job, everything.

At least the shame, combined with a sickening realisation that I'm going to have to buy this bloody borrowed drysuit, then burn it, kills the hiccups. And that hopefully is all anyone else, including Nigel and his video keen learners, will ever notice. Although when it comes to general observation skills it's clear that the group scores well, seeing as half of them seem to know all about Ellie's bionic leg. Whereas I still can't see anything different about her in the photos they shared.

Later Nigel says I'm welcome to come back and repeat the last little bit – those rescues of unconscious paddlers, swimmers and so on. I mumble a reply, a bit rude really, but today's been crushing.

I'd been warned that everyone falls for the coach. Not me: instead of developing a crush, I leave this training weekend totally crushed. No certificate, little sense that I've improved and a backpack of embarrassment that means I can never go on a course here again.

And there's no way I'll forget today given that I now own the damp orange drysuit, which I will only be able to wash clean after a serious search session on Google.

In a taxi on the way back to Horsham train station as I'm trying to find a way to stop my wet booties and BA, casually packed into a big Sainsbury's bag, dripping on to the seats, Jack's familiar voice suddenly bounces out of the cab's radio. I look around surprised, and then tune into what must be an ad. Jack's saying: "Because I'm out on the water all day, every day I need my vitamins. That's why I count on *Dutch & Barrett Sporty 7s* to keep on making a splash. Race you to the bridge!" I'm guessing radio production times are quicker than TV, and you don't have to look as good, but wow that is a shock – paddling Jack a radio star, even with a nail through his foot.

The irony is that the only thing that will make me feel better about today's misadventures is to go for a paddle.

9. PEACE ON THE WATER

Lara makes an early start

I'm lying face down on my board letting my right hand drift in silken water. It's the sort of summer morning where you just want to relish being outside, doing not much. I tuck my paddle out of the way and breathe deeply as if I was into yoga enough to not muddle up this little mantra – *smell the coffee (breathe in), cool the coffee (blow out)*. I've overheard Flame saying it often enough in her yoga classes, but today I plan to take it literally as I've put a Thermos filled with hot coffee under the bungee straps, to drink later. It'll be my treat.

Although at 8am it's early enough for the towpath users to be rushing to work or getting some Strava kilometres in before they settle at their desks, there's a real sense of peace where I am. The weather reports say it's going to be oppressively hot later. But now as I turn over, eyes half shut against the powering-up rays, it's easy to chill. I breathe in deeply then exhale with as much force as I can manage. Greg used to say that my yogic breathing made me sound like an asthmatic swan. I push the thought of my missing man away and let my board drift into an umbrella of willow leaves. This is my happy place – a green domed room full of filtered sunlight where I can secretly tie my ankle leash to the NO MOORING sign and try to relax. And even if I can't, I'm out of view of the converted architects' office with its mix of modern glass and warehouse vernacular, and out of the way of any early boats chugging towards the lock.

If you were judging just how relaxed I felt, you'd probably give me a strong 7.5. Struggling to sleep I've got used to brain shut down, but after the Surrey lake debacle it was whirring with painful self-rescue self-criticism until now. The mix of young coot chirrups from the nest to my left and gentle quacks of Mrs Duck and her chain of fluffy tabby-feathered ducklings in this hidden space, alongside the steady fall of water as it drops over the sluice by the lock is so calming that slowly, very slowly, I start paying more attention to the rocking of the board, then the gentle tug of my board meeting and losing the bank. In the distance I can just hear happy barks as the dog walkers of Graham Street Park lob balls for their pets. A sun-warmed blue damselfly flits across the water and lands on my hand, expertly finding a sunny spot despite the filtering of the willow branches. The wind tickles the leaves and breathes a sweet kiss on to my bare legs, feet, arms and face.

A few more seconds and I'll be asleep: the humiliation of soggy drysuits and the stress of Flame's SUP business contest forgotten.

Or I would have been if – crash – some tall idiot in a black polo neck hadn't paddled straight into my willow tree bower, hitting my board. He's shunted backwards by the willow branches, scrabbles to hang on but then yells as he falls with a shockingly noisy splash into the shady depths. The metal Thermos and I are rolled off into the canal, and as I shoot my left leg downwards, my foot gets squeezed into some kind of metal trap. Thankfully my head stays above water, and as, unlike my assailant, I'm wearing a buoyancy aid (amazing what that Surrey safety course taught me to notice!), I've got something on that will take the strain out of floating. But unlike him I'm snared, so I can't clamber back on to my paddleboard. Perplexed, I just hold the side trying not to think about what must have got my foot. Annoyingly the coffee flask has sunk.

Meanwhile the idiot is thrashing around.

"Where's my paddle? Why are you doing nothing? How do you get back on this stupid thing anyway?" he shouts half-coherently. Even if I spoke he wouldn't be able to hear over his furious paddle scrabbling. This paddler is now trying to wriggle himself on to the tail end of his board. He must think it's working as he starts to kick his legs wildly, hitting the coot's nest with his foot as he slowly edges himself up the steeply-angled board.

"Stop!" I shout.

Every kick takes him a fraction further up the board, but also whacks the nest sending a baby coot up in the air and then plop into the water. It would be a funny 1970s cartoon, but this is wildlife decimation in real life. Given that I'm stuck like a mouse in a humane trap there's nothing I can do except watch the horror show.

At last, he's back on his board. An untidy, apologetic fool. "You must think I'm awfully rude," he says, still breathless. "I'm Simon. Just got this board and I'm finding it a struggle to get used to it. No one I know who paddles mentioned that you had to actually learn to use a raceboard. Didn't even mean to go under the trees. No brakes. No idea how to turn, but at least nothing is broken." I glare at him, furious that he's unaware of his own coot attack. He stops his monologue and looks at me suspiciously. "And you, are you alright?"

"I've got my foot stuck in a shopping trolley or worse; watched coot carnage and been given a dunking. OF COURSE I'M FINE, absolutely fine." I think I say this in my head – it is still the only bit of me he can see – but whatever he hears seems to send him into panic. I see him feeling around for his phone – he has of course got it thoroughly soaked when he toppled in. I can sense his horror as he realises he's lost his contacts. Hear him about-turn clumsily and splash paddle to the opposite side where he stops a jogger on the towpath and asks where's the nearest open cafe. Apparently he needs to get his SIM card and battery into a box of dry rice urgently.

I shouldn't have said I was fine!

Fortunately the jogger peers in my direction and notices that I haven't got back on my board. I think he shouts something at me, but it's hard to hear. I try to tread water with my other leg, very cautious in case it gets stuck in the metal trap too. I don't think I'm going to drown, but it's weird to be tethered by my leg.

Time moves slowly, but not so long after the jogger details my potential drowning predicament to the emergency services I catch hold of the rickety NO MOORING sign, upending it, oops, but somehow still manage to drag myself (and what turns out to be a shopping basket masquerading as a man trap) on to the slippery bank under the willow tree. Disturbed, this quickly becomes smelly. It's also an unnaturally green colour, perhaps something to do with nightly dollops of goose poo. I'm not sure why the coot family thought this was decent real estate potential, although I guess on the canal the supply of wildlife "housing" spots that can't be disturbed by dogs, cats, paddlers, boaters or passers-by is extremely limited. I'm sure if the architects ever found time to leave their canal-fronted office for a five minute sit down by this willow they'd have devised some kind of waterbird latrine.

Eventually a fire engine arrives at the nearest canal bridge and six firemen run up to assess how to rescue me from their side of the towpath.

"Alright love?" booms a fireman through a megaphone. I give a thumbs up, probably hidden by the willow. Simon, the rubbish paddler, must have sorted out his phone as he now turns himself "helpful" and offers his board to the firefighters. Sensibly they turn this down. An inflatable dinghy is pumped up and launched, then its 15 horse power engine powered up.

Now four firefighters, all in helmets, are intent on rescuing me, though they've certainly picked the slowest boat on the canal. They look a bit stunned when they emerge under the willow branches and realise that I'm 100 per cent alive, that clearly wasn't the message that got them speeding through red lights with sirens on. But they cheer up when they realise that my foot is properly jammed in the basket.

"Get the cutting tools out," orders the fireman nearest to me.

Their little dinghy makes a shockingly slow return trip for the right kit. I think embarrassment can stop time.

When this is all over I resolve to clear more litter from the canal as my way of apologising to the poor coot family which thankfully seems to be back together. I can see that the black hen and her steel grey-feathered chicks with their pleading open mouths are now busily begging for a snail and seed breakfast.

The paddleboarder is convinced he's a hero and has saved my life, although me and the jogger (now probably clocking into Teams on his laptop) know better. The emergency services have enjoyed making a real canal rescue. And the passers-by have fuelled up on the drama, aided by takeaway cups of coffee from the *Buddleia* Narrowboat Cafe. If this was a novel it'd be the start of a watery version of *Pride and Prejudice* because I think paddleboarding Simon is the most idiotic man I've met on the canal. I expect the coot mum does too.

Once my foot is noisily released from the wire basket I thank the firemen, mumble more thanks across the canal at the rest of the team, then stick the broken basket on to my board and paddle back towards the Boat Club, picking up discarded coffee cups and bits of plastic as I go.

There's a shocking amount of litter in the canal. Until today I'm not sure I'd noticed it. Perhaps I was too busy balancing to look around.

"How wonderful of you to organise an impromptu litter pick on this beautiful morning," says Bio Queen leaning over the *Buddleia* Narrowboat Cafe's deck with camera in hand filming my finds. I wave and smile as if I've just been on a scheduled litter pick for #OutdoorSisters. Normally, praise from random people on the canalside about my ability to actually stand up on a paddleboard is a welcome ego boost, but today, from the sharp-eyed Bio Queen it feels more sinister.

Distracted by chasing litter with the side-edge of my paddle blade, I don't notice that I've paddled into the end of an early SUP yoga class being run by Flame. Forgetting her warning about never interrupting the *shavasana* (that move at the very end of class when you lie down and fall asleep/mimic a corpse) I call out "Good morning." Half a dozen seemingly dead women twitch into action. Some sit up, most respond with chirrupy good mornings as if they've turned into waterbirds. Flame looks at me in disbelief. But the damage is done – the class's yogic focus is lost – so she grins herself back to the present, thanking everyone for the session and wishes them a happy day.

"That's such a nice way to start the morning," I gabble trying not to mention my ignominious early morning bath and shopping basket battle.

"Hang on Lara, I can see you'd like to talk, so when you've showered and warmed up, let's get a coffee together when I've finished up," says Flame possibly holding her nose (she's downwind of my goose poo-stained tracksuit) while helping her clients to detach from the yoga line – an ingenious way of keeping paddleboards still enough (even in a 10 mph wind) for clients to try those crazy SUP yoga poses. Honestly they don't even mind doing their poses while standing backwards on their board.

Heading into the showers Gladys bustles past me with her mop. Her eyes widen as she says, "Good morning to Lara who looks like she's been in the callaloo soup again…" which inspires me to take twice as long in the shower. Hopefully a really thorough soap will wash off the grime.

*****

Of course we go back to the *Buddleia* Narrowboat Cafe.

"How was the weed on that sunset paddle?" asks Bio Queen in a crocheted summer dress covered in bells that makes her tinkle as she walks around her empire. I can imagine Jack would think this hilarious, but Flame definitely is in awe. "Did you make it yourself?" she asks.

"Well what do you think?" responds Bio Queen staring at me. We are definitely having a multi-layered conversation. I'm ready to fess up about the whole brownie mess – and how Jack sort of doctored the incident report – but Flame has fortunately misunderstood Bio Queen's heavy handed hints.

"Yes Lara – you need to remind me to get on to the Canal & River Trust. We need their cutting boat up here now that it's high summer. I think duckweed can double in size every two or three days and there are some patches of floating pennywort too – so if it all expands with the weather this hot we'll soon be walking on the water, not paddling," she says laughing at the thought. Bio Queen raises one eyebrow at me and mimes eating something small. "Shall I get you your usual then?" she asks us.

"Coffee and cake would be fine," I say with a faint shiver as if I'm still in wet clothes after today's ducking.

Bio Queen waltzes over with a tray of pastries. "On the house, 'for the shock'," she says to me.

"That's kind of you," answers Flame ducking whatever hints Bio Queen is lobbing at us. Then she starts laughing. "Oh Lara, you are funny. We all know!"

My false smile freezes.

"If you fall in the canal and get stuck in a shopping basket and then get rescued by the fire service, do you really think someone isn't going to tell me or Bio Queen?"

I'm so relieved that she seems to only be up to speed with today's debacle that I sigh with relief.

"I think I might have been making your life stressful," says Flame, sipping her oat milk latte. "And I'm sorry that up to now I haven't been able to reassure you more, face-to-face, I'm just so busy, you know how it is. But if you've got the time now, maybe you could share how your business development plans are shaping up?"

Wow. I hadn't expected this sort of grilling. Half choking on my coffee I catch a deep breath.

"Oh you do that cool coffee mantra, nice," says Flame warmly.

"Yes, um. I've been learning to fall," I say hesitantly. But my words are drowned by a clattering from the cafe gallery. This feels like an inquisition, unexpected and rather like being held underwater. Part of me needs to come up for air, which is hard enough on this humid summer day. The other part is just trying to hold on to whatever life ropes are being sent to my aid before real damage happens.

"Learning to fail?" says Flame, puzzled.

"No fall. You know, just like what's just happened in the kitchen." I gesture wildly towards where Bio Queen was probably juggling plates, but the woman has already moved back to our table and instead I brush her bare, freshly inked arm.

"You like my new tat?" says Bio Queen approvingly, even though she definitely flinched. It must still hurt. "I'm doing a pop up tattoo shop later this month, you'll have to give the artist a try. Just like me."

"It looks sore," I say at the same moment as Flame says, "Cool". Bio Queen laughs and goes back to her tasks.

"OK, let's start again," tries Flame now that it's possible to hear each other.

"Well I've got a to do list, and I'm to doing it…"

"That's funny," laughs Flame. She clearly thinks I'm joking.

I scrabble through what perhaps I should be doing to win a business, and then surprise myself, and possibly Flame, with some proper jargon. "I've been talking with my mentor" (cross fingers she doesn't ask who, as it's Gladys) "and I am working up a development plan that I can share with you on Google Drive later. I've tried to do some financial forecasting and it's looking good. I thought more litter picking would be quite zeitgeist," I say struggling to pronounce this word, before adding lamely, "Yeah, I'm really on it. And enjoying it. Yeah."

Flame puts down her phone where she was making notes and focuses on her cup.

"That really sounds good Lara. I wasn't sure how much you were into this, but now I'm super confident that you really do want to take #OutdoorSisters to the next level. That's great news. And I'm so impressed that you've got a mentor, such a powerful move."

"Yes, true," I nod sagely. "But actually I do have some questions for you about the timeline." (Ha, I had no idea that I knew that word, 'timeline'). "When's the handover supposed to be, as it will really help with my business projections?" (I'm on a roll).

Flame stares at me, still perhaps shocked that her incompetent older woman SUP 'pet' has just used language the start-up generation can understand.

"Well we can do a sliding transfer with Companies House and the bank etc, but I think the main switch would be around the time of the Canal Festival… Oh gosh, sorry, gotta pick up this call," she says looking at her vibrating phone. "I hope you don't mind, as it's going to be a long one. Thanks Lara, let me pick up the tab. And I'll be in touch soon."

I smile happily. And I really mean it. Flame has put me back in the race. Even better, Bio Queen overheard it all. Take that Ellie, limping Jack and the mystery contender.

.

10. LITTER PICK

Lara and Dizzy supervise clients from an art collective including Martyn, Sky, Valentina

Now it's August, Flame doesn't seem to come to the Boat Club anymore, but she still finds time to send messages. "Hi (waving hand emoji). I've got a good session for you. There's a collective of artists who want to clean up litter and then photograph it for an exhibition. There's quite a big group so Dizzy will need to come along with you. Hugs."

Dizzy! I had no idea she could paddleboard or would ever join us litter picking. But with a big group I'll definitely need her help.

Dizzy has her headphones on when I rush breathless into the Boat Club. There's just half an hour to sort out the boards, paddles and buoyancy aids. While I collect up enough buckets and trugs to gather the rubbish we will find in the water and tiny planted areas, Dizzy adds a pop of air into each board. When she sees me looking at her surprised, she briefly pulls her headphones back to explain that, "I've done all this stuff before at university in Southampton when I was in the paddle club. That's why I told Flame I could help out if she ever needed it," before retreating.

Phew, that means she can probably help out with this paddle successfully as our canal has neither tides, currents nor massive ferries.

Two months into the business contest and I have a nasty feeling that Flame still doesn't trust me out on my own with clients. It'll take a long time to live down my rescue failures on the sunset paddle. I wanted to chat to my friend Adebola about that total disaster as she's good at strategy, but because I'm always working on weekends and evenings, when she's out socialising, her phone keeps cutting into an annoying Giffgaff message to "leave a message". I've resorted to stalking her now on social media, just to check she's not dead or left the country, like Greg. But she's definitely in London. Insta is full of her clinking glasses in fancy bars and hipster pubs. It looks as if she's going out even more than she used to. That'll be something I can find out when my SUP schedule calms down and we catch up in September for a much-delayed meet up. It's my fault really, as while the weather is hot and sunny Flame's SUP clients are keeping me busy. But I'd like to talk to her about what happened with Greg too. It feels really strange that he's totally disappeared. And being in India when the new football season starts seems an odd choice.

I can't feel sorry for myself for long when I'm near paddleboards, plus the artist collective are hilarious. Introducing themselves they all provide their name, artist tag and pronoun. It's clear they'd rather talk art than risk their pink and blue hairdos reaching for litter. I think they'd be happy to spend hours explaining their vision and values, but Dizzy and I gradually get them fitted into buoyancy aids and assign leashes and sunglass straps.

There's a lot of chatter about Turner Prize winners of some big art comp which goes over my head, so to get the group's attention I ask if anyone heard the big storm last night.

"The lightning was amazing," says Martyn. "I'm a property guardian in a church that's just about to be converted and spent about an hour watching the storm cross London from the tower. There was a proper forked lightning show before the thunder brought the rain."

"Well, that's official then, you are definitely a zombie unless you wear your yellow hard hat and rubber shoes in that crumbling space," jokes another. I look hard at the first speaker, the property guardian squatter. There is a certain zombie-look to him, very pale skin and hair. I wonder if zombies can swim and what the ethics are on rescuing them.

In contrast Dizzy is totally on task. She quickly helps the group move from pontoon to kneeling on their boards, but out of the corner of my eye I see her stepping straight on to her board like a surfer. That's super dangerous to try from the canal's hard cement sides – unless you do it very confidently, just like her and then it looks cool. I hope our artists were too into their own chatter to notice or copy her. Fortunately it's the latter; they are busy fretting about who'll be the first to collect a full trug of 'trashspiration'.

The wind is pushing our boards along at around 8 mph – faster when it gusts – towards the very end of the canal where there are certain to be piles of McDonald's packaging. The artists love the grey urban setting, ringed by skyscrapers, contrasting with this rather shabby bit of nature so close to Old Street. Out come phones and notebooks (let them not fall in) to capture the swan's discarded big white feather trapped in a sinking Big Mac box; the green duckweed turned to slime that pours out of an old cola bottle and a quantity of plastic prosecco corks that blue-hair snaps up.

"We knew Islington would have the perfect litter," says Sky/Skyways/they, wearing a GoPro, who seems to be the person who booked the session after meeting Flame on a Thames beach down by the Tate Modern.

"Valentina and me were looking for clay pipes on the beach, but Flame's puppy kept digging; showering us with pebbles and wet mud which made the task hard and kind of forced us to have a chat," continues Sky gesturing at the blue-haired woman who I now realise sometimes works at Bio Queen's cafe. They then tell me in some detail about the history of clay pipes, ignoring all my curious questions about Flame's 'fur baby'.

Turns out the zombie artist is also a friend of Bio Queen, so the collective will be heading to the *Buddleia* Narrowboat Cafe after their litter pick.

Martyn/mArt/he is obsessed by crisp packets – searching them out like a missile and then reading the small print to check the year of production. "A good crisp packet is like a bottle, it'll survive for years, though unlike a fine wine the contents go off. I'm told the plastic can last 30 years." He waits for me to be impressed, but I've been working on the canal for long enough to know this fact. In return I tell him that if disposable nappies had been around back in the day, then we might still have King James I's nappies. He sniffs as if inhaling super century baby poo.

"That's awesomely revolting – we better rename our trash show to something like Wholly Shit," jokes Martyn. "Wait there's another," he shouts, excited by the chase, and paddles off towards a tangle of fast food wrappings and a sun-bleached blue Walker's cheese and onion packet brought up to the surface by someone else's sweeping paddle stroke. The canal's never more than two metres deep but it can apparently turn up all sorts of crisp surprises.

I overhear Dizzy ask where the show will be, but the artists don't seem too keen to give us an actual date and place. "We'd have to kill you if we told you," says someone busily scooping out pea-sized pieces of polystyrene packaging with the sort of excited squeals you'd make if you unexpectedly discovered enough pearls in a puddle to make a three-strand necklace.

After half an hour with so many litter pickers at work this bit of our canal is transformed. It's just so annoying that the bins by the water don't close properly, so that whenever there's even a breath of wind anything at the top of the bin is just blown out and ends up in the canal. Here it drifts around waiting for a litter picking squad to clear it; or is swallowed by the canal's long-suffering wildlife (especially the youngsters who haven't yet learnt plastic from prey) or, just as bad, slowly sinks.

When the water is silt-free and sunlight catches the bottom you can just see an array of discarded fizzy drink cans. We pull up a couple and find they're mostly flattened. "I reckon an alien would think we carpet our canal with aluminium cans," says one of the artists. "It makes me want to drain it and get digging."

"Well she's clearly got trashspiration from being out on the water. The Arts Council will love this, " laughs Martyn, paddling back towards me triumphantly clutching a three-year-old Hula Hoop packet.

We drop off a couple of trugs full of rubbish and then head in the other direction, past the *Buddleia* Narrowboat Cafe so Bio Queen can take a few snazzy photos of this art collective from her narrowboat and where the blue-haired one leaves us as she's late for her shift there.

By the time we paddle past the pub our artists are getting bored and over-confident. Several are standing up mock play fighting with their litter finds; one has paddled into the lock base to get some extra rubbish and is deaf to our 'come back' cries thanks to the noise of water trickling through the old wood gates. Thankfully when Sky spots a suitcase bobbing around in the water the gang comes together.

"Is it a heist? Or a lover kicked out? Or carelessness?" we puzzle looking at the black travel suitcase, with its little roll-along wheels and pulled up carry handle incongruously floating near the Bridge of Sighs. Sky pulls it on to the front of their board, scattering their haul of crisp packets. We all watch, back of the neck hairs prickling, as they unzip the suitcase, by now imaginations at full stretch – expecting a sawn-off shotgun, horse's head or worse.

An aeroplane drones slowly above the Regent's Canal and the alder branches seem to rattle as we hold our breath for what turns out to be an anti-climax, or more accurately rather like a bad trip to the laundrette. "It's dry!" shouts Sky.

"But what's in there?" we ask, craning necks.

"Some jilted bloke's shit – passport, bank statements, benefits letters. He's not paying for his kid," says Sky slowly sifting through the suitcase. Eventually Martyn and Sky agree that there are no crisp packets in the suitcase, so another of the collective takes possession for their own art-litter haul. Finders aren't keepers with this group if the find doesn't match your theme.

I take some photos of the next best things the group has retrieved: a spoon, plastic panda and a clear plastic bread bag holding a crocheted red rose. There are innumerable bits of sweetie wrappers plus empty plastic energy drink bottles and biodegradable coffee cups. Secretly I think this is going to be a rubbish, rubbish art show. But I'm also glad the canal is a lot cleaner.

Dizzy paddles over to me, still with headphones on. She points at her wrist where I see she's got a Garmin watch – the ultimate sportsperson's training tracker and the exact model that Jack told me he needed to buy to boost his performance. It's an odd thing for a DJ to need, I thought they were more for the truly sporty. Anyway I don't think I'm going to need one soon, as I can't figure out what Dizzy's Garmin numbers mean. Instead I look at my own waterproof wrist watch with its trusty hands. As always time has just disappeared on the water. We have to get the artists back on land so they can sort out their litter treasure, recycle, log and record the brands and then clean up, otherwise they'll run off leaving oily brown marks dripped out of upended tin cans and duckweed-leaking packaging staining Flame's boards.

As we paddle back, the sun high in the sky, happy with our haul, the group begins to look around and notice the area better. When I brush against the water mint and yellow flag iris that are growing by the canal edge, Sky suddenly asks who is chewing gum, presumably catching a whiff of mint. A nest on a half-sinking boat near the Boat Club jetty has three just hatched coots and their red and yellow spiked feather hats get a lot of admiration. Just as someone starts to imitate David Attenborough's voice and pretend that we're in a wildlife documentary a couple of gulls steal the show. At first we think they are checking us out for easy pickings, like chips or an ice cream, but then they fall into a screaming dive towards the coot's nest and with incredible speed one snatches a nestling. It carries it back towards the tower block mobbed by more of its sharp-beaked seagull friends. Above us the chick is torn to pieces, food for feathers higher up the food chain, and we all saw it happen. As an inspiration for a compelling art work, that piratical dinner dive can't rank much higher, but seeing nature red in tooth and claw is upsetting, even for artists intent to shock and awe.

"Can't believe we saw that." "Horrible." "Nasty, nasty nature." "I feel sick."

"I know it's shocking, but gulls do this from time to time," says Dizzy, cucumber calm. I make a mental note to be on her side in any argument from now on.

"Why don't you move the nest?" "Does that always happen?" "Can't we save the baby?" "Will the others be safe?" "Why are the seagulls inland anyway?"

There are a million questions from the artists which I just can't answer. Flame runs litter picks to make money from people keen to virtue signal. The herring gulls, in their science-lab white feathered coats, using skyscrapers like cliffs for safer nesting and street lights to rifle through litter bins for longer hours, don't mind being cast as the James Bond baddies. It's odd to think that for most of the year the gulls sort carefully through the discarded packaging that people wanting a 'quick' drink or snack leave behind, making them the canal's top litter pickers. I just wish they wouldn't celebrate by picking off a newly-hatched coot chick. Even if it is unwrapped.

11. BACK AT THE *BUDDLEIA* NARROWBOAT CAFE

Lara and Dizzy witness a makeover

"Do you want to sit inside or out?" I ask Dizzy as we walk towards the *Buddleia* Narrowboat cafe for a quick cuppa before the next litter pick Flame's organised for this afternoon. At least I don't need to worry about a lack of rubbish as with picnickers, MaccyD fans and the too few bins overflowing with coffee cups and gins in tins, the canal and basin will certainly provide enough rubbish for any number of litter picks.

Dizzy nods, which doesn't help me at all.

"It's probably the first time we've really had a conversation. You always seem to be in headphones," I try. "Oh!" I gasp sharply as Dizzy looks at me as if I was one of those hungry gulls swooping on the nesting coots, "that's not really a question is it?"

Dizzy laughs dryly. "I'm doing a lot of studying – business stuff. The headphones means Mami cannot trickle in. She'd expected me to get a job the moment I graduated, not to keep on paying out to learn."

"So why do you come to the Boat Club, couldn't you do your studies somewhere a bit quieter or further away from her?" I ask, surprised – though not as surprised as when Flame sent over another WhatsUp to ask if I could cope with one more litter pick for a corporate group today and again work with Dizzy for support. Clearly Flame knows that Dizzy can SUP, even if I didn't and to be fair Dizzy's always sporty-looking in her tight gym gear and lace up runners. Perhaps she practises on the water when

I'm not around as she's definitely at the Boat Club more than me.

For a long time I've wondered why Gladys with cleaning buckets, Mr Sheen polish and microfibre cloths is followed from room to room by her daughter, but however I ask, Dizzy politely dodges the question. Eventually she finds a way to wrap up my nosiness with a more direct response: "Well Lara I have my reasons, if you see what I mean. And it's no hardship being there with her. Just like it's no hardship being here with you."

I give her a sharp look, but I don't think Dizzy meant this in a mean way, and there's no point taking offence when we could just have a quick snack before we need to get organised for our next paddlers.

But Bio Queen isn't keen on letting us sit and chat quietly. What she wants to do is talk about her makeover of the *Buddleia*. The blue-haired artist gives me and Dizzy a wave. It's Valentina who sometimes sleeps on board, in exchange for cycling up to Lidl to bring back supplies in a sort of navigational version of Paris's Shakespeare & Co. Despite her busy morning litter picking with us (a pile of prosecco corks and plastic bottle tops are drying in a trug by the cafe gangplank) she's ignoring her damp clothes while enthusiastically upending the sewing machine trestle tables then piling them haphazardly on to the towpath. Those heavy metal objects were never a great choice for a cafe with such limited space, the span's only two arm widths wide, but I'm impressed Bio Queen is willing to let things go. She even chuckles when one of the towpath dog walker's French bulldog gives the discarded tables a sniff and then brazenly urinates on what until yesterday were her oh-so-treasured tables.

"Paddle ladies that was a brilliant session and I'd like to do a litter pick again," says Valentina huffing past with a box, "but I'm now focusing on the next makeover for Bio Queen, so I can't really chat."

Delegating allows Bio Queen to strike a pose and run her own chat show. Today she is in storm wear, what one might describe as her lightning strike outfit: a vibrant planet of blue blouse and an even bluer skirt. Around her neck is an industrial monster – what look like old-fashioned metal toilet chains worn as necklaces. She's topped this with the bluest velvet beret adorned with a sparkling three-pronged trident brooch. Clanking and rustling like an unseaworthy vessel in a summer storm she loads a tray with two oat milk lattes and a pile of her like-to-shock dead fly vegan pastries (made with booze-soaked raisins not insects) then guides us towards her new table and chair arrangement. To be fair this looks more like an upturned supermarket shopping basket, with a couple of cushions provided for comfort. I'm not sure anyone will be able to sit on them for more than a few minutes, which is going to make it hard to linger in her cafe. Worse, her new wire tables have a distinct slope (just like a shopping trolley which is of course what they have been repurposed from, making it impossible to put a mug down without it sliding. I nurse the cafe's canal-style big tin enamel mug, over-heating my hands and fearing it'll burn my lips if I dare to take a sip, while Bio Queen prattles on…

"I've had such a great idea, inspired by my neighbours," she says brushing off icing sugar from her kitchen apron. "I'm going to revamp the cafe and my friend USP will document it all ready for the Canal Festival. It'll get people talking about the Trashspiration show, on and off line, and some might even promise to go zero waste."

Bio Queen is just the sort of woman to already know what the art show is called, and to have a friend called USP.

"He's a podcaster with a studio down at Old Street. When I first met him, years ago, he was a teenager at the Boat Club busy saving the whale, so nothing's changed much!" she laughs. "See what I did there with podcaster?"

"Clever," says Dizzy suddenly, "but it's not that visual doing a makeover on a podcast. How will it work?"

Bio Queen gives both of us the sort of dirty look Icelandic and Japanese whalers reserve for Greenpeace activists.

"Actually, you ladies will probably like USP, he's got a paddleboard and sometimes goes out on the canal. In fact, he said he bumped into you Lara, the other morning up by the willow tree, surrounded by firemen."

There is an awkward silence and then as I lift my mug moodily to my mouth I stupidly burn my lip and yelp.

"Easy tiger," soothes Bio Queen, squeezing herself beside me to stare into my mouth. I do not like the way she invades my personal space. "It's nothing, just dab some butter on that burn. Actually I'll do it for you." Which she does – though with a vegan spread which I hope will work – and then gets back to her makeover story. Phew, no more about me in the water again for a bit. It's still too soon for me to find it funny.

"So, I've sold the treadle machine tables on Facebook Marketplace for a total song, and some lovely woman from Surbiton is picking them up when her boyfriend's borrowed a van. Then Valentina and I are going to make every table and chair on board like this one you are trying out, rescued from the canal. What do you think of that?"

This is not a question she really wants answered. Once Bio Queen has an idea then we've all learnt to just wait until she's moved on to the next obsession.

I look again at the wire mesh my still full mug cannot balance safely on. We knew already, but she's now pointing out that the cafe's new tables are blatantly rusty shopping trollies with the wheels removed, just like the one I got my foot stuck in.

We sit in silence for about 45 seconds, until I ask, "Um, does Sainsbury's mind?".

"Hahahahaha," Bio Queen cackles. "August April fool! Well you know, Lara, we all saw you getting stuck in that metal shopping basket, even if you want to forget, and once we realised you weren't going to drown it was probably the funniest thing we've ever pretended not to witness on the canal – up there with assignations, arguments and celebrity spots. And didn't you get lucky with all those tasty rescue crew swarming around you intent on saving your life? I just had to commemorate the show with a little joke of my own so USP helped me set this all up," she adds as the podcaster, sporting the same sort of high neck black jumper he wore when he knocked me off my board, but this time with black jeans, a rather French Left Bank look that's far too hot for an English summer day, idles over to bump fists.

"Lara, nice to meet you again," he says, all smarm. "I hope you've forgiven me by now for losing your Thermos and making you swim – gave you a good anecdote anyway. And Bio Queen has filled me in on Flame's business challenge from her ringside seat," he adds, acknowledging Dizzy with a raised finger, "so I can do an interview with either or both of you. Any time! The studio is so close."

This sounds more like an order than an invitation.

"I'll ask all the big questions, anything you want," he continues. "As Hegel said, 'nothing great has ever been accompanied in the world without passion', so let's talk paddleboarding passions."

"Nice approach," says Dizzy looking him straight in the eye as if she knows him of old but still doesn't rate him, "and what sort of things do you think Lara can tell you?"

"Answers to all the big questions," he repeats before striding off towards the counter to help himself to a slice of gluten-free banana and beetroot cake.

"He really does the Existentialist thing well," I mutter. This second meeting hasn't warmed me to Simon aka USP at all. Plus he's got a daft name.

Bio Queen ignores the tension, moving on to her good community ideas. She's starting to focus intensely on the Canal Festival which is traditionally held in the first weekend of September. "Can the Boat Club help out with some have-a-go SUP sessions? What do we think of the Trashspiration theme this year? Is it strong enough girls? It's been such odd weather – searingly hot for wildlife and the canal – and there are already talks of hosepipe bans and general confusion about whether this should be called climate change or global warming," she says leaning over us, "should we focus still on litter or move it up a gear to tackle end-of-the-world as we know it themes?"

Dizzy looks out of the port window towards the Boat Club. I smile weakly, mouth full of dead fly cake.

Bio Queen pauses for a moment, looking as if she's going to share a secret. "The rumours are true ladies, I intend to remove all the old canal nick-knacks," she picks up a jug painted with blooming roses as if it is a rotting fish to help illustrate her point. "By the Canal Festival I should have styled the cafe to match the unseemly side of urban life. I thought maybe once the new tables are in we could 'decorate' it with Islington road kill? I've got a friend who is a taxidermist, he works at the Get Stuffed shop on Essex Road, so not too far away. Anyway, he said I could borrow a few founder creatures – he's got a nice red fox missing half a tail and a nuclear rat family (Mum, Dad and 2.2 ratlets)." It's all sounding quite serious until she strikes her hip (I take this to mean as below the belt) and asks sweetly, "Perhaps you and Jack can help supply the runover cats?"

As I look at my feet, still in wetsuit bootees, Dizzy starts to giggle.

I can't imagine that a tiny cafe with supermarket trolleys as tables and road kill as decoration is going to be popular, but I certainly don't want to let on to Dizzy more than I can about Jack and the cat (cats!), given that clearly Dizzy and Flame are far friendlier than I'd realised.

It's so hard keeping up with who knows who in this tiny waterside world.

USP comes back to our table and we all listen to Bio Queen outline her scaring-the-community plans with literal litter literacy (an alliteration I think numbly) using art, until she eventually stands up and says, "Anyway, drinks are on me today and you two better run – she gestures to me and Dizzy – as I can see your next victims are waiting at the gate." She points out of the little narrowboat windows still fringed by fairy lights and leggy spider plants outgrowing their old olive oil tins, towards the Boat Club, then whips our mugs away. I look where she's pointing and realise that this seat really does have clear sight lines, almost as if she moored her boat right there to keep her eye on us. Neither Dizzy nor I have managed to drink more than a couple of centimetres from the burn-your-mouth mugs, nor arrange a podcast date.

I know it's petty, but I've found a crack in our reuse and repair champion: Bio Queen definitely needs to sort out food waste generated on board her boat.

12. FANCY DRESS LITTER PICK

Lara and Dizzy bond running a corporate litter pick.
The clients are all dressed as famous artists.

We can see the next group standing stressing by the locked Boat Club gate, clearly worried that they're never going to be let in. But as we speed walk along the towpath towards them, Dizzy suddenly gets talkative.

"It's that coffee Lara, that's what's done it. The smell of undrunk cups reminds me of all those waiting around and paddle times at uni. I had this lovely friend who got me into SUP, but when we graduated she took a job doing SUP yoga and sunset tours for tourists over on Koh Samui. She was good enough for the GB racing squad, so such a strange decision," she says, almost apologetic.

"I guess you miss her?" I ask sympathetically, though I'm also thinking of my missing in-Instagram-action friend Adebola.

"Well not Holly so much now, but yes, the whole 'team water' atmosphere. It was so supportive. At this Boat Club it feels so different, like a job you do for pay, not a life. The #OutdoorSisters clients expect us to look after them and Mami looks after everyone. No one helps pack away the boards or asks about us. Like what we want to do with our careers," she says, hand creeping towards her brown eyes.

I take Dizzy's other arm gently. "Don't cry. It'll get better. The year after graduating is always tough. My daughters have just gone through this too. Everyone seems to be getting on to the work elevator faster or they're better paid, or whatever. Just don't compare. You'll suddenly launch, you'll see." I try to sound enthusiastic, but my fingers are crossed. It's not just rough finding the right role in your early 20s, it's hard keeping that career trajectory up in your 50s. There's just as much job insecurity to cope with (all those short-term contracts and rejection letters still hurt) plus regrets. If you haven't got to be head of department or a CEO you start feeling edged out. I thought running a project was OK, it took up enough of my life, and the kids took the rest, but it was no safety net at all. And then Greg went. Life comes down to just a trio of big worries – somewhere to live; paid work and someone who's got your back.

If she wasn't crying I think I'd be.

We both need distraction and this second group of litter picking artists will surely give us that. And that means we better speed up…

Dizzy seems relieved to have to break into a jog. Unlike me she can run and talk. She reckons they can't be like the last group of *real* artists because this group seems to be mostly checking their phones in a sort of 'someone's going to pay for this because they're not yet here' way that people working in tech, or the City, and equipped with a strong interest in value for money tend to hold. They do seem to be dressed up though – could Flame had booked us a fancy dress party?

"Oh no USP is joining our thrill seekers," mutters Dizzy raising her left pencilled eyebrow (just like her Mum) towards the polo neck podcaster as we hurry up to our next group.

"Hello again," says USP, arm outstretched, half smiling as if he might bite. Dizzy's phone tumbles on to the ground in what seems to be a very obvious move to avoid being touched. Uncomfortably, I offer my own hand instead, which by now is encased in an outsize red gauntlet ready for the litter pick. When he feels the rubber his mouth tightens and he shakes my hand hard enough to hurt. It's strange as Bio Queen's friends are usually a bit more informal. And we were only talking to him a moment ago at the Narrowboat Cafe.

"Do you know this gang of artists," I ask him politely, struggling not to puff. I would also have liked to ask Dizzy privately what the problem is with this man, but now she's turned her back to us both and is busy checking her phone for damage, or dialling an execution squad.

"Yes, they are mostly architects who work in the offices at Old Street above my studio. It's quite funny as two of the guys are also called Simon, like me, but as I wasn't an architect they gave me the nickname of USP, an abbreviation for U are Simon the Podcaster. I thought it was funny until it stuck. Anyway, a better question might be, do *you* know them?" USP chuckles.

I look closely at the group of fancy dress and try to guess who is who. By luck art is my joker section in pub quizzes. I think I can spot Salvador Dali (with Hackney moustache), Frida Khalo (with a monobrow), Alice Neele (in dark leggings but she's cheating a little by pinning a couple of easy-to-recognise portraits to her dark blue jumper, with the ensemble crowned with a navy feather in her hair). Andy Warhol (in a Campbell Soup jumper), David Hockney (flat cap and blue glasses frames) and Van Gogh (with part-bandaged head) are instantly recognisable. No one seems to be Picasso, perhaps his womanising makes him less popular for modern dressing-up taste, but there is a woman clutching a cardboard cut-out of a battered violin case which seems to belong to Picasso's good Cubist friend Georges Braque.

There's one left who has long brown hair and is wearing a red white and blue floaty dress with trainers. Saying nothing, mouth clamped shut, she holds up a flyer for a cleaner on one side and John Lewis' bedroom furniture on the other. Dizzy looks baffled but then starts to laugh, before guessing, "this must be that artist who did the unmade bed." So we've got Tracey Emin too, though this Tracey's enigmatic expression suggests we've either got it right or she's moonlighting as the Mona Lisa.

"And we brought along USP as our dealer," jokes Andy Warhol. "Art dealer. You know, like Jay Jopling from White Cube."

This afternoon is going to be very tiring I think, smiling at Andy Warhol and USP through gritted teeth.

Maybe the 'dress as an artist and go paddleboarding' idea sounded fun when it was dreamed up as an office away day, but I'm not sure our group are so keen to go on the water now that they are faced with a canal that needs its plastic sandwich wrappers and drinks bottles removed.

It seems they're simultaneously worried about falling in and fears that their colleagues' panic antics won't be recorded to TikTok quality.

Dizzy and I hand out buoyancy aids and then duck into the office to plan our second litter picking route of the day. It's also a chance to squeeze out a few more puns to lob to our 'artists'. We come up with 'art attack', 'artful dodger' and 'rubbish art' before giggling to a halt.

"But seriously where are you all from?" I ask our Tracey Emin, who needs the buoyancy aid adjusted as it's far too loose. She laughs and says "Margate", which sets the group off into giggles. At the moment our fake artists seem very similar to the real ones, a bit reluctant to get on the paddleboards.

"No, really most of us were in my Margate project team last year," says Andy Warhol self-importantly. "Did the woman we booked this with tell you that we're architects? Anyway as we work nearby we decided to put a bit of hero power into cleaning up our local canal." He's interrupted by Salvador Dali, who maintains such a terrible Spanish accent throughout that he's basically unintelligible. We find out that Dali needs to leave by 4pm, Alice Neele has a gadget monitoring her diabetes, which must not get wet, and Frida Kahlo is extremely fearful about falling in.

"It'll all be fine," says Dizzy, taking charge. "The trick is to kneel on the paddleboards, with your knees either side of the handle. We always start on our knees so there's no danger of hitting your head on the concrete canal side, but if you do fancy standing up, try and keep your feet still and on either side of the deck handle. And face the right way round! Once you're kneeling on the boards me and Lara will put your litter trug on the front. We thought you might like to start picking litter up right away, but let's try to stay as a group."

This is only Dizzy's second session for #OutdoorSisters but she knows so much, you'd have thought she'd have been coaching for years.

The artists are now kitted up in buoyancy aids and gaudy washing up gloves to protect them from litter lurgies. Their leashes are on. And finally they are kneeling on their boards and heading towards the *Buddleia* Narrowboat Cafe. The gulls are circling above now, making me feel like I'm in a horror movie, but our group says it reminds them of the seaside – and Margate. I don't think this would be a good moment to mention the recent coot attack. Besides there's a gentle breeze behind us which will soon blow us towards what we want, rubbish.

First find is a Coca-Cola can, the easiest of pickings, but next is a lost child's toy – a plastic panda which is found by a joyful Andy Warhol (I'm amazed we've found two on the same day and wonder if our earlier real artist friends threw it back). Frida Kahlo, gaining confidence as she gets into the chase, shows real rubbish art potential as she exclaims at the variety of crisp packets semi-submerged in the water. These are so satisfying to hoick up from the depths with the paddle, if you can get the blade lined up the right way. If you can't then it's a game of catch until they are successfully flipped into the trug or the cheese and onion branding flashes gleefully, like a fish that got away, as it sink-spins to the bottom. By the end of the session, and despite the morning clean-up, she's sure to have a variety of soggy Walkers, McCoys, Hula Hoops and Quavers packets spilling out of the battered blue litter trug on the front of her board.

Dizzy and I exchange glances – I just know she's thinking the same as me, Frida would get on well with our last crisp obsessive, Martyn.

Everyone else has gone for the potpourri approach and scooped up everything and anything, including loads of little bits of pesky plastic that blow off when you tear and unwrap. There are also plant pots, a bit of old rope, two full cans of cheapo cocktail, several cable ties and a fluorescent yellow lighter.

The worst part of any litter pick is logging what we find quickly and sometimes having to sneakily recycle what we've collected. These architects are rule followers and say that anything found in the canal is apparently contaminated. If we had time to dry things off, then we could probably recycle a lot more – especially as there's a supermarket nearby that has a recycling bin for plastics only. The other problem is a good one to have, trying to get litter pickers to stop collecting litter when we ask, for some reason as their eyes adjust to seeing the reams of litter bobbing around the canal they seem to get totally into it and are reluctant to pack up.

I try and distract the nearest paddler by pointing out a coot. As the bird is about 30 metres away and my client clearly has no interest in wildlife I switch tack and start to chat about narrowboats. "What would you call your boat?" I ask cheerfully. Hockney suggests Prince2 which seems to crack up his friends. I see USP smirk, adding that, "you'd expect that sort of name from project managers, especially ones who prefer to work from home." I have no idea what he's talking about. But Dizzy the business studies student seems to find it funny. Maybe I misheard.

This group is ready to have a go standing before we disembark. But none of us, and especially Flame, had anticipated that today would be the day a sewage release would be making its slow way via a storm drain into our canal and on down to the Thames.

When unlucky Frida knocks her trug with the paddle she lurches forward to rescue the tipped out crisp packets and suddenly starts squealing.

At first we joke that she's having an 'art attack', but it's clear she's not found a fun bit of litter. What's upset her is spotting a little pod of disgustingness – a couple of condoms, two wet wipes and a flotilla of greasy ear buds.

Then Hockney retrieves something similar. But browner. It is in fact much, much worse.

Alice Neele – absolutely out of character now – starts to cry when she finds she can't figure out how to turn around and paddle out of the gunk and back to the Boat Club.

USP, who seems to be a lot better at stand-up paddleboarding than when I first met him, perhaps because our club boards are a bit wider, paddles over to the Bermuda Triangle of yuck. "From up here I can see the water is a browner shade," he says, "and it stinks." We all watch as his face turns a thunder-cloud purple, it's obvious he's angry, but no one expects him to then snap at Dizzy – or maybe me – that, "You really should have known this would happen, there was a big storm last night, wasn't there? Well that's when the water companies do this. This was always going to be risky and you're the one who should be making these calls now. That's why I'm investing in you." He turns away as if trying to control his temper, muttering, "At least it'll be good for the podcast."

Tracey Emin has been just ahead of the main litter pickers and now she gives a yell. "Dead fish!"

"Shit there are fish in the canal?" sobs Alice Neele poking her paddle in unhappy circles through the green and brown lottery of slime, "I absolutely can't bear fish. How can they be alive in this awful water, in this awful place?"

It is definitely intended to be a rhetorical question. But USP from his lofty viewpoint of 5 foot 11 inches on his paddleboard tells us that it's not just one fish that's had it, all over the surface of the City Road Basin are floating dead silvery fish. And tragically, sailing through this carnage is our pair of swans.

Something terrible has happened to the water.

I overhear Dizzy muttering to herself, "Oh my days, he's started the bullying all over again," though later she insists she was just saying some of the dead fish are dace.

It's clear this session has to end right now, but getting our unskilled group to turn around and paddle back through the stinking sewage and dead fish bodies is traumatic. I've never seen anything like this happen here on the canal, although of course you hear about sewage releases all the time. The wild water swimmers and fishermen are always moaning. Now I understand why.

Dizzy, grim-faced, says she's not seen it here before either, but then paddles off mid-sentence to help Alice Neele.

I now know that Flame's catch-all advice is that if people are worried about pollution from contact with the canal water then they just need to drink a can of cola. "It kills all known germs, yes even the low sugar version," is the phrase we're told to use to stop the trots. But back on shore with the images of dead fish and faeces flashing through my mind I feel like a modern Lady Macbeth – not even the most expensive Jo Malone tester could rid me of this afternoon's stinking memories.

To compound today's stresses the Boat Club showers refuse to provide proper hot water. So, we have to send our report to the Environment Agency hotline number using our still sewage scented hands.

"Well thank the stars that no one fell off," says Dizzy as we hose off the boards and tidy up. "But expect a little light colonic irrigation tomorrow. Seriously," she adds, "and that's not a fun thought."

I look at her and can see she means it. We started this session feeling sorry for ourselves, now that canal belly seems inescapable, we definitely feel worse.

13. YOU COULD WALK ACROSS THE CANAL

Lara is taking out clients: Hussain, Muhammed, Ahmed

It's already the second weekend in August and the towpath is crowded with couples and little groups of friends heading to Broadway Market. The early birds are smugly flowing the other way, laden with weighty loaves of sourdough, street food picnics and huge bunches of flowers wrapped up in newspaper. It's years, decades actually, since I walked around as a loved-up couple.

For a mini-second I see myself at a long Sunday brunch and bookshop binge with Greg, but it's like looking at an old-fashioned sepia photo from another century. I turn towards the sun, screw my eyes shut and tell myself to just stop it. Thankfully I'm too busy to let the pain in as I'm on my way to the Other Boat Club, located in Hackney. This is where I'm meeting Muhammed and his friends for a gentle paddle.

Flame's known the guys for a while, they're all South Somali heritage who've spent time as teenage asylum seekers. They may have the right to stay but they have almost no money, so holidays are out. Flame says almost anything fun for them is out, not because they don't want fun – they definitely do – but because of their cash crisis. Any money they have goes on booking the artificial-grass football pitches near King's Cross. In fact that's how they all became friends. Their sometimes football coach is one of Flame's yoga retreat clients, so when Flame heard about how hard it was for the guys to try new sports, she asked if they'd like to have a go paddleboarding, and then applied for a grant to get them out on the water. The aim is to train a couple to be coaches, but it's baby steps for now and the guys are just enjoying that strange feeling of standing on a board to travel along the middle of this London canal.

Flame and I took them for the first trip out and had a hoot – they were all quick learners and it was definitely different hearing Arabic being spoken as we paddled along Regent's Canal. Five of the original 12 guys were really keen, explaining how this was a great way to forget all the troubles of their lives.

I knew exactly what they meant – paddling an inflatable SUP board is almost meditative, but when you've just started and are trying to stay balanced it's also impossible to focus on anything other than being on the board. If you've got a problem, from as minor as how to pick up a duvet from the laundrette before it shuts (to get rid of the aftershave smell that makes you cry), or as pressing as where to find enough money for the weekend's meals, it cannot nag for your attention while you're trying to balance on water.

I've never told Flame about Greg's absence, that's why it is a genuine miracle that she's kept me so busy this summer, allowing me to forget the horrible cruelty of living without him most of the time. It's not exactly him that I miss, it's being in a couple. I don't think I'd have coped without the #OutdoorSisters shifts and a business plan to work up. With a shudder I try to imagine myself stuck at home sending off unanswered job applications to do something indoors that I wouldn't enjoy and probably wouldn't pay our mortgage. No, it's too horrible. I exhale loudly (that's the cool the soup breath) and bring my focus back to today.

All the guys in this group ticked the box saying that they can swim. I looked at a map and saw that Somalia has a very long coastline, though how you'd get to learn to swim when there's fighting or, as in most of their cases, as an asylum seeker in London with absolutely no money, must take ingenuity. Luckily our buoyancy aids fit even the tallest of the guys, so they'll be safe whatever happens. Actually, Hussain, at a towering 1.9 metres, should be able to keep his nose and mouth above water, if he's unlucky enough to fall off, because our canal really is not that deep.

Flame likes clients to wear an old pair of trainers or beach shoes, but the guys don't have spare kit. Instead, they take off the trainers they are wearing and use Hussain to place them high up on top of the sloping tin roof covering the recently spruced up kayak shed. No one but a seagull is going to see or steal them from up there.

"OK if you're not wearing shoes just be careful of the goose poo (which is very liquid) and broken glass (which is very sharp) if you have to walk along the towpath," I say firmly as we move across the grass towards the pontoon below their A-frame club house, thinking how lucky I am to be wearing water shoes.

"We'll be fine," reassures Muhammed, laughing as he chats to a new member of today's group, Ahmed. Their star striker! I'm always saying that paddleboarding is the world's fastest growing sport, but when it comes to this little amateur football squad it's demonstrably true.

Footballers learn fast. I'm not sure Ahmed is prepared to fall in, but after prodding the mud on the canal floor with the paddle blade, which stirs up a squirl of sediment, he says with clear relief, "I can feel the bottom," and then stands, last one up. Soon the group is gently paddling towards Acton's Lock, only stopping beside the Hoxton

Docks studios to watch people installing a giant fibreglass shark in the water.

"Did you see the size of that shark?" I ask just as Ahmed, with his eyes glowing, says, "Did you see the hot chick?"

We're clearly looking out for different things.

I turn my head in the direction he seems to be staring and just see a glimpse of a blonde woman throwing shapes on a hoop dangling from the beam of the warehouse's ceiling, several metres off the ground. It's shadowy indoors, but weirdly, she looks just like Flame. Perhaps that's a Millennial thing – all sporty 30-somethings have a multitude of skills besides their well-known love affair with endurance challenges and avocado?

What would it be like to be 30 again? I'd be in sculpted leggings, on a juice diet, looking forward to eating something delicious with friends tonight, where we'd go wild and order too many Baby Guinness as we dream up a daft project (like placing giant model sharks in the canal), then stay up dancing to our friend the DJ's set until 3am. I'd be chatting about my latest ultra-distance paddle project and the drawbacks to social enterprises getting listed on the Stock Exchange... "Can you remind me to stop here when we come back?" I say dreamily to Ahmed in an attempt to get him paddling along the canal again, though I'm certain that he won't need reminding.

Our paddle is lovely: gentle splashes, laughter and a chance to see the canal from different eyes. The guys have no interest in the history of the place, what they want to know is practical: how much it costs to live on a boat and the location of the fruit and flower market. They also ask if there are always so many people on the towpath on a Saturday.

Despite four identically dull council tower blocks, the streets behind this bit of the canal – and even the council housing – are totally gentrified by Hackney hipsters with their groomed beards, clop clop boots and swishing pony tails. Even so, there really are a lot of dressed-up party people about today – perhaps waiting for a flash mob to start? There's also the sort of pent-up atmosphere that you get at the start of a festival when everyone's just arrived: excited for a weekend with the bands, the race to find a camping spot, and then chilling with that first pint of Camden Pale Ale or drug of choice.

We turn around, and on our way back to the Other Boat Club things get complicated.

Ahmed starts to slow down (he's tired) and Hussein speeds up (he's nailed it). Muhammed, still standing, stops at the big old wharf by Hoxton Docks clearly transfixed by the girl on the aerial hoop who seems to be doing a public show alongside another woman who is a proper gym bunny, running through the hardest of the cool yoga moves – headstands and backbends – with incredible ease. On the opposite bank people are milling around watching these contortionists.

It's not that easy for anyone except paddleboarders to stand and stare at either the aerial performance or the yellow-hatted workers installing the mega shark models, as along the towpath, pushing through anyone who's halted for even a second are groups of young people with blow up boats trailing pumps and clinking bags of not yet drunk cans.

"It's lively on this bit of the canal isn't it?" says Muhammed approvingly. I look at the performers moving on the hoop from splits to no hands and then at the yoga aficionado and wonder if this is a Flame and Ellie double-act. Suddenly I spot Jack on the side of the warehouse dock and realise it must be. What are they all doing?

"Hi," I yell as loud as I've ever shouted. Jack seems to notice as he gives a cautious wave in my direction – perhaps the vitamins he's endlessly advertising also help with hearing – and then turns back towards yoga Ellie, or whoever she is.

Embarrassed by being left out by the Boat Club SUP team, I suggest to the group that we should paddle on. They tear themselves away from the show reluctantly. The wind is in our favour, pushing us along, but once we get under the low brick bridge the canal water seems to have disappeared, replaced with inflatable dinghies in every colour.

"You could walk across the canal just using the boats," observes Muhammed. That's really the last thing I hear my group say as the combination of police helicopters (they've sent two) buzzing above, heavy bass pulsing from the narrowboat closest to the bridge and hundreds of people partying on the canal and towpath, drown out any chance of instruction or conversation.

We're in the middle of what seems to be a summer canal rave by joyful London invaders.

Anyone not dressed in onesies and peaked sailor hats is in their skimpy best. Clearly people knew this guerrilla event was planned, even if it's surprised me, as there's a bloke leaning out of his house boat *Tinkerbell* selling helium balloons and at least three people in a red canoe piled up with boxes of IPA and Fosters' lager making a noise about having a card machine so "you can buy your booze here".

With the wind pushing us we suddenly run aground into the invading party boats which are slowly coming towards us. It's chaos! Now there's a narrowboat, horn sounding, coming through regardless, simply pushing any vessel it meets out of the way, whatever their size or flimsy manufacture. I try and tell my guys to get on their knees, but they can't hear (or see my signals) and as we're forced out of the big boat's way, we paddleboarders are split up on either side of the canal.

A woman stands up in the inflatable dinghy beside me to wave her tattoo-covered arms at a friend and immediately tumbles into the water. "Man overboard!" she shouts emerging with dripping makeup and a missing set of false eyelashes before trying to drag her boyfriend into the water. He avoids a bath by dunking her with his oar, playfully. Soon I'm in such a total melee of dancing boats and tipsy drinkers that there's no way I can reconvene my little group. I see Muhammed on the bank give me a thumbs up as he mimes holding a phone, but then he's gone. Not long after I watch a guy dressed in a lime green mankini and Captain's hat reclining solidly on one of the #OutdoorSisters paddleboards as he's lifted up and across the canal like a Roman emperor.

Panicking, I ring Flame for help. Of course her phone's on message.

The fun on the water is infectious though – "Here have a beer". It's a proper party so I try to forget my lost clients and lost boards. I'm sure they'll turn up again.

Not everyone is happy: the people who live on the canal's normally private west bank are out in their back gardens getting furious whenever a boat reveller struggles up their side for a landlubberly jig. One empty garden has been turned into an impromptu pee den. The moorhen that lived just below it has had its nest trashed.

This Canal-ival is a total takeover of the neighbourhood.

Somehow I reach the Other Boat Club still with my board and paddle, but on the way I got a telling off from a grey-haired Canal & River Trust official who saw my big buoyancy aid and clearly thought I was part of the organising floating festival crew. "That's next year's ambition," I say rudely, surprised by his verbal attack and distracted by seeing three minibus loads of police, in riot gear, start to arrest everyone caught up in the Canal-ival. Until now I hadn't realised there was a them and us split amongst canal users, though I was beginning to clock that wildlife have the least voice as they are always at mortal risk of dogs off lead, watersport beginners, big boats passing, towpath picnickers, walkers, exploring toddlers, cyclists – everyone.

In her self-appointed role as Canal Festival director Bio Queen is always imagining the canal as a rave venue. She'll laugh when she discovers that I got trapped with my paddlers like a nut in a chocolate bar at the impromptu Canal-ival, especially when I pretend that I really loved it.

Whatever her Trashspiration art show plans, I'm sure next month's official Canal Festival (approved by the Canal & River Trust and licensed by the council) will have better press and far, far less arrests than the Canal-ival.

14. STORM LIGHT

Lara and Flame mic up for USP

It's strange to be wearing neoprene leggings walking through Old Street's Tech City, where casual smart is the dress code, and to actually be with Flame away from the canal, but she wants me to help her out with the famous podcast. In fact she insists I come along, even offering to pay me for my time, because her original wing woman, Dizzy, is still struck down with belly ache and diarrhoea after that horrible sewage experience. Thankfully no one else we took out for the litter picks has reported symptoms, although if the fancy dress artists are anything like me they will have spent most of that night, and the next, awake imagining the misery of ear pain, stomach cramps, nausea, rushing to the toilet, finishing the loo paper and finally – the ultimate humiliation – failing to find a public toilet.

I really don't feel up to doing any podcast. Flame thinks I'm reluctant because I don't much like USP, whom she calls Simon. Hopefully that annoys him as much as his pretentious Hegel quoting irritates me and Dizzy (yes, I'm speaking for Dizzy).

"I know you had a bit of a clash with Simon, but he's a solid chap most of the time," says Flame on our rather rushed way to the studio, simultaneously revealing that she really does have the eyes and ears of the community.

"Was it Bio Queen who told you that?" I ask a bit huffily.

"Yes, but Simon had already let me know. He can be clumsy, but I reckon this studio chat should be fun. He's got quite a good set up and a lot of listeners, so it's also good publicity for what we do," she says almost inaudibly over her shoulder. I don't want to run to catch up as I'm going to sweat in these neoprene leggings, but I also don't want to get lost either, so I uncomfortably chase Flame as she paces through the IT workers, apologising frequently to the ones who are attempting to balance a take-out coffee and talk on their phones as I brush past them. Flame is going so fast that I have to half jog, hoping not to be pushed under the traffic or into someone's arms. At last she stops at a set of glass doors grandly placed between big stone pillars and rings the bell.

We're buzzed in.

It's so much quieter off the stressful City Road. We soon find ourselves in a converted office on the second floor which has become an air-conditioned, soundproof studio – at any rate all the windows are blocked out.

There's a big rectangle table, with microphones at eight settings which is a bit daunting for the promised simple chat. The moment USP sees us he passes us both a set of headphones, eyes on his phone's timer. "I'm just so delighted you could come today Flame and, um, I don't actually know your full name, but you seem to have escaped the algal bloom lurgy," he says looking at me directly.

"And this is Derrick who is in charge of the buttons," continues USP pointing at the other man in the room who looks as if he might be USP's retired Dad, which is quite sweet. Flame seems to know the old guy too and sends over a little air kiss as she's now trapped in place at the studio table by cables. That's probably the only way to make her stop moving and listen, unless she's in one of those super difficult yoga poses.

"So this is how it will go – our theme tune music, a couple of jingles and then we'll get going after I say, 'This podcast was brought to you by Tunnock's Caramel Wafers'," says USP.

"You've got Tunnock's sponsoring you?" I interrupt, slightly confused by this detail. Surely polo neck wearing existentialist podcasters don't eat Scottish trail snacks? They're for the rest of us to enjoy.

"No, that's Simon's dream," laughs Flame, "until that day he's got to put up with boring old vitamins from Dutch & Barrett. OK let's do this as I've got to keep to time today, long story…"

And just like that, the music blasts around the studio, the jingles play and USP turns on his version of podcast charm.

"Well, hello, today we are delighted to have Flame and, um, her colleague, from #OutdoorSisters, EC1. This central London paddleboarding club is the place to hang out in the summer. And your host today, and every episode, USP, can tell you that's 100 per cent right because I've been there often."

"Hi USP, "says Flame in a smiling voice, making it clear at once she's a media natural. "Me and Lara are just so happy to be here."

"Well as Hegel says, 'We learn from history that we do not learn from history.' Flame, you've had three fabulous years working your waterproof socks off with canal adventures and yoga, so what's new?"

It's a shame this isn't TV as USP looks genuinely interested.

"Plenty! I'm going to take some time out for a secret project, which I can at least hint to you will be about Blue Water theory, and how inner city blue spaces like the

Regent's Canal are so healing for people's wellbeing. But right now there's a not-very-serious contest to see who's going to be the new me. We've got some fabulous candidates including Lara. In fact there are three women and one man – any one of them could run #OutdoorSisters, but I want to hand it over to someone who just gets what we do," responds Flame. "What's happening now is a low key trial where all the candidates just run the sort of sessions they think will work best and also share their plans for growth with me. It's been keeping us all very busy."

I definitely hadn't realised that bit about the club expanding. Knowing that I haven't figured out, let alone shared any ambitious plans with her, the hair seems to prickle at the back of my neck. I thought I was taking this taking-over her business seriously, but clearly not at the level Flame has just outlined.

I look sideways at Flame's notebook and see a series of SWOT grids in her neat handwriting. It's impossible to miss.

Who to take over #OutdoorSisters?
June (approx)
Lara
Keen
Bit old?

Ellie (my mini me!)
Skills are good
Gets marketing
Too like me?

Jack
Skills - very good
Is he too blokey?

Chevelle
Business degree
Bit stand-offish

July
Lara
Why did she say she was learning to fail?

Ellie (my mini me!)
Too busy?
Not sure she's that interested

Jack
Skills - very good
Keeps customers alive
Reliable and also unreliable (that cat saga)

Chevelle
Just not sure

August
Lara
Got enough time but does she give off a desperate vibe?

Ellie (my mini me!)
Possibly #OutdoorSisters is a bit small for her ambition

Jack
Got to trust my gut

Chevelle
Definitely gutsy, and talented but Simon???

"That sounds like a scene from one of those Shakespeare tragedies," USP is saying as I finish sneakily reading the SWOT. "You know when King Lear tries to get his daughters to tell them how much they love him, and then things go terribly wrong. I'm guessing our other studio guest today is either a sweet Cordelia or a vicious Goneril or Regan figure?"

Flame looks daggers at me – she's seen what I've just read – and then at USP. "Well that's a bit far-fetched, this is more trial by doing, and it's been *fun* for everyone. You've enjoyed it haven't you Lara?"

Thrown by the question – and revelations – I start to cough, buying myself a bit of time. Who the hell is Chevelle on Flame's list? The nice older bloke hands me a glass of rather warm water, which thankfully allows me to figure what to say next. Keep it simple! Focus! Laugh at the host's jokes!

"Funny!" I say as warmly as I can into the mic. "Yes, I love paddleboarding and Flame's got a very particular set up that works really well for Islington and the sort of people who live around Old Street – the artists, architects and web developers and well, people from everywhere," I say thinking of Muhammed and his friends.

"We can fit people in before and after work, or any time, and quickly give them the skills to safely get on a paddleboard and take relaxing exercise…" At this point my first rush of inspiration has gone, I'm an unemployed fundraiser and a paddleboard assistant, not a soundbite puppet. Floundering, I wind up by stating, "We keep people safe, our priority is safety…"

"And fun," adds Flame slightly sharply when she realises I've stopped talking.

"Yes, safety and fun, hardly an oxymoron," USP draws the two soundbites together, possibly being rude, possibly just a proficient podcast host. "So paddling on – hahaha – is it difficult to paddleboard? Have you ever fallen off Flame?"

"Well not deliberately, but I have of course been into the canal – we take pride in how clean the water can be," says Flame, perhaps stressing the words 'can be' a little too much. "And that's why we also run litter picks every week of the season. Obviously we then recycle what we can, but we also are trying to encourage the cafes along the towpath to promote reusable cups, so the cup you buy your tea in doesn't then end up in a towpath bin and just blow into the canal at the first puff of wind. Because if it does it will probably go down to the River Thames, damaging wildlife and the look of the water along the way before it goes out to sea. It's a disgrace really when you think all you wanted was a nice cuppa, not a wild-world-destroyer."

"Yes, the state of the canal has become a big issue recently. But we'll go into that another time," says USP grimly. "For now our listeners need to know that Flame is SUP-erb, apologies for that pun, irresistible, but she really is SUP-erb at balance which is why she's also an aerial hoop artist, yoga teacher and paddleboarder coach. What about you Lara, you seem more like the rest of us landlubbers, how did you get into this crazy balance sport, is it all blue water zen for you or do you still fall off?" asks USP. He's definitely not being as friendly to me, but I smile and reply as if I'm a sunny stand-up paddleboarder (which I mostly am).

"Actually it's yoga that got me into this. I started with a lesson run by Flame," I remember, hesitantly recalling the chronology. "Now I'm pretty good at standing on the board and looking over either shoulder to help clients or take photos, which everyone loves, but I've had my moments getting soggy. Do you know that one crazy paddler actually ran into me a few weeks ago, upending me and themselves?" USP, recognising himself, grins, but doesn't interrupt.

"Generally on our lovely bit of canal it's about one in 20 that is unlucky and plops into the water. As I'm often dressed in wetsuit top and leggings, I'm going to be dryish, and as we provide everyone with a buoyancy aid, even if you fall in you're going to be safe and keep your head above water." Remembering Flame's comment earlier I then tag on squeakily, "We make you 'be safe and have fun!'"

How did that come out so clunkily? And I stupidly forget to add that every booking gives the Boat Club charity a little donation towards the kids' club, the over 60s paddlers and a disabled group.

"How's the new boss recruitment actually going now the three month contest is nearly up?' asks USP, starting on another tack. This question is obviously for Flame and she answers in considerable depth about what she's looking for – experience, qualifications, real Blue Water passion etc, etc. As she speaks I realise that I'm actually not her dream successor. I can feel my heart start to beat twice as fast, as if I'm close to a panic attack. I take a big breath and try to focus on nice things – mist rising off the water, the proud swan parents with the three cygnets paraded between them, big clumps of yellow king cup growing by the graffiti wall. A tear rolls down my cheek and at exactly that moment the dreadful jingle starring Jack fills the studio… "Because I'm out on the water all day, every day I need my vitamins. That's why I count on *Dutch & Barrett Sporty 7s* to keep on making a splash. Race you to the bridge!"

It seems this jingle is the signal for USP to wrap up the show. Flame looks at me in shock. She must think I'm very strange about Jack's success. I struggle to pull it together by taking another sip from the glass of warm water.

"And so this week on *Listen with USP* and the *Wholly Shit Show* thank you to our guests Flame, and her colleague Lara Lake, and all our sponsors, but most of all to our listeners. We hope you can get yourself down to #OutdoorSisters and the upcoming Canal Festival and have a go trying out the magical canal we live besides. Have a good one. Over and out!" USP holds his trigger finger to his lip, nods his head twice, as if thanking his audience, and then removes the headset.

We all wait quietly until he's unclipped the cables. But instead of an end of show chat he gets up and walks around to Flame's chair to pack up her headset before giving her a gentle kiss on the cheek. When I stand up he offers me a clean hanky, saying, "No proper freebies today, sorry ladies! But thank you for helping me make a great show. Good stuff in that. I'll see you at the Canal Festival if not before with all the planning that's going on. Now you ladies better get out of here as I've got a very strange character coming in for another interview about the festival, and if she sees you she'll definitely get distracted."

"Surely you haven't got Bio Queen to leave her cafe?" I say croakily, trying to sound as if I wasn't crying a moment ago.

USP just gives me – or maybe Flame – a very big wink.

Flame zips towards the exit, leaving me chasing her again. "Are you going back to the Boat Club?" I ask. What I really want to know is why she's used me as the also-ran in this business race, to make it feel as competitive as the over-subscribed Hackney half-marathon, but I'm not feeling strong enough to ask.

"No, I can't get back again today, but Lara we do need to talk as I need to know how you lost the clients and all their boards yesterday. The problem is that right now I've got to catch the train and get back to Pericles." She holds up her hand to stop me from saying anything, "Yes, that's my puppy and yes he's just adorable. I'm not even sure I've had time to show you or anyone at the club pics of him. It makes me so happy just thinking about my cute boy, so could you just ping me a voice note about what went on," she says heading towards the tube station. "See you, that podcast was a lot of fun, just like Simon said it would be. We did well, most of the time. Speak in five…"

I really need a coffee, so pop into Pret, guiltily accepting a disposable cup, and then head back to the Boat Club. I reckon I'll sit on some steps in the sunshine at the head of the City Road basin, well away from the hubbub of Old Street. I've probably got enough battery to apologise and explain how I came back to the Other Boat Club with no clients yesterday. More crucially I need to get back into the race: if I'm not running #OutdoorSisters will any of the other clubs employ me? How will I cope without weekends spent paddleboarding?

Today nothing wants to go quite to plan, even the sit spot where I choose to type my side of the story to Flame is shaded by a newly sprouted giant tower block. From being too hot, I'm now distinctly chilly.

"Well, I didn't really lose Muhammed, Ahmed and co," I tap to Flame over a WhatsUp line dipping in and out of connection. "It's just there was suddenly such a huge crowd on the water that the, um, clients, got too far away for me to be able to talk with them. But they were all over 21 and I think they had fun."

This last comment is definitely true as Muhammed sent me a couple of WhatsUp later with photos of him enjoying mayhem on the canal. In one he's standing on top of a narrowboat pretending to fight a bloke in a tricorn pirate hat, but his big grin gives the stunt away. He's also sent a couple of seconds of video. In this he's waving in the Royal style from an inflatable, behind him is pandemonium – couples kissing, beer cans being shaken then lobbed into the Canal-ival festival crowd and a great wave of song including cheesy, happy snatches of *Hi Ho Silver Lining* and *You are the Sunshine of My Life*, and behind that the thud, thud, thud of the big bass the Canal-ival organisers presumably brought along. That's when I see a flash of Jack behind a megaphone. I wonder what him, Flame and Ellie were all up to at Hoxton Docks? Why didn't I ask then? Or Flame just now?

"It's just not good for #OutdoorSisters," responds Flame typing. She says she's had to deal with a furious Canal & River Trust rep tear into her because a couple of her branded boards were filmed in the mêlée "It made it look as if #OutdoorSisters had been part of the Canal-ival organising crew, which was definitely an illegal rave, and that meant I had to join the volunteers clearing the water and towpath for most of last night. Hundreds of those inflatable boats got left behind and they were left full of empty tins and discarded fancy dress," she adds in a voice note. Understandably she's shattered, and not too happy with me.

I walk to the Boat Club and get enough signal to call her.

"I am sorry, it was a weird experience, and the guys are adults. I was wondering what on earth I'd have done if it was the Nature Club primary school kids on the boards," I say cautiously.

"Well thankfully it wasn't! I'm sorry too, but this is what I really wanted to say: I don't think it's going to work out, you running the club," says Flame suddenly getting harder to hear. "It's not the Canal-ival debacle, there are other things."

For a moment it sounds as if she's going to name them, and then she switches her tone back to the positive Flame I know best. "Look you've got loads of life experience, but your water sense is a bit hit and miss. I want to be fair too, and so this is hard, but I need to tell you that there's something else that's changed my mind. One of the other possible candidates has found a way to invest some money into the business and I think this approach has to be a lot more sustainable. You know them too, it's…" And of course, just at the big reveal, the line goes absolutely dead.

I sit down on the Boat Club's rickety picnic bench, unusually covered with drinking bottles and banana skins, then take three deep breaths but still the tears start to prickle. For god's sake, crying twice in a day. I feel like I've left the planet, sitting dazed. After a bit I'm able to take another deep breath and start to half hear the Egyptian Geese squabbling on the water. A fly buzzes around my face then leaves.

Dizzy, face set, walks past me with a mop and bucket in her hand towards the men's changing rooms, she's brave being here in her weak bowel-ed state, though at least she's close to multiple toilets. The main gate bell rings, and no one moves to open it. Everything is normal at the Boat Club, and yet everything has changed. My whole summer of trying to get a completely new career together has just collapsed.

Matching my mood there's a sudden slow rumble of thunder.

I close my eyes and think of the lost weekends and evenings taking people on to the canal; the endless reassuring of the nervous; the money I've spent upping my skills; the humiliations and tasteless coffee at the *Buddleia* Narrowboat Cafe. I feel so furious with the world that avoids employing older women, and then even when people really try to kick start a new career – like paddleboarding – those in charge fail to value people like me because we came to the water world too late. That's it, I'm going to cycle home.

My employment battle is hopeless: I'm too old, too new, too unskilled and in this final twist, too poor to take over a tinpot paddleboard business that's only open for six months of the year on a scuzzy bit of e-coli-riddled canal. Yeah, I'm lucky to be out of it. From today my social life takes priority.

I'll call Adebola and ask her to help me set up on Tinder. The thought makes me laugh and at that moment Jack in an oversized polo shirt with Great Britain emblazoned on it saunters over to the bench.

"You look like you're having fun," he says nastily. I gurn, what an idiot. "USP ask you out did he? The old puffed up git's got a bit of a hero complex. Always wants to date the useless girls – that's why Dizzy hates him."

I've never heard Jack being face-to-face rude before. Shocked, I ignore the insults to me and perhaps Dizzy. Instead, trying to stay calm I point out that: "Flame doesn't hate him."

"You're going down a really weird road now Hashtag Outdoor Sister. Him dating her would be incest," snaps Jack angrily.

A wet sponge comes flying across the yard and lands splat by Jack's feet. "A near miss," I say looking down. "Not next time," retorts Dizzy, this time lobbying another dripping sponge successfully at Jack which lands with a wet smack on his hip. "Stop being rude and petty Jack just because we disagree about the cross bow turn," she shouts walking towards us, adding, "You certainly don't take Flame's heart-to-hearts well. It's clear she's turned you down..."

"Me too, about half an hour ago," I burst out and pat Jack's arm.

Jack's left eyebrow folds down momentarily and then he laughs out loud. "You bloody stirrer Dizzy – and miserable muddlehead Lara. I'm still in the #OutdoorSisters contest. Doubt you guys are. And for the record, it's officially the cross over turn."

Dizzy takes a 20p coin out of her pocket and walks over to a pale blue car I've never seen before which is parked by the kayak shed. "If this is yours Jack I'm so going to key it. But right now, I need your help, Mami isn't well and we've got to get her to A&E."

15. AWKWARD TOUR

Lara and Ellie take a long paddle with clients including Ahmed and Lulie

Every paddler loves an adventure, but I am not in the mood to join the Big One. This planned #OutdoorSisters trip takes us down the canal past Haggerston, Hoxton with its Canali-ival memories, then left to Hackney Wick and finally swinging along the River Lea Navigation and into the Limehouse Basin where the water escapes into the Thames.

The Big One is billed as a proper jolly: all our regulars turn up ready to enjoy a paddle challenge, hopeful of a following wind and just the right amount of coffee and cake stops. This year we're planning to picnic on the grass by the London Stadium where West Ham play. I think this might be why football fan Ahmed signed up. Anyway, weeks ago I'd said I had other plans, but have again failed to pin down my friend Adebola so I am again around, and now also suddenly needed because Dizzy is still suffering. Discreetly she calls it "tied to the toilet", meaning that she can't risk such a long trip without adult diapers, which no one wants to wear. Reading between the lines I reckon Dizzy is fine, but that's her cover story while she tries to sort out Gladys' health.

Given yesterday's post podcast shock reveal that I'm not her successor, I'd like to think it was an apologetic Flame who messages me to 'please, please, please' come along on the Big One.

"Yes," I message back, knowing I'm a doormat.

But a long paddle on a summer day is also just what I need: sunshine on my back and in my head, plus the sounds of the quiet slap of my paddle and regulated breath gradually numbing all brain chatter from the physical effort of 30 strokes a minute for six hours.

There's no way I can think of mice nights, absent Greg or my dud social life when I'm paddling.

Flame has also promised me a full day's pay, which is truthfully what stopped me from saying a sulky no. The fact that I might find out some of the questions I have about Gladys' health and what Flame, Ellie and Jack were doing hanging around (literally) at Hoxton Docks is just a bonus.

In a rush I search for my dry bag and pack it with tasty carbs, sun cream and two refillable water bottles.

By the time I reach the Boat Club it's pandemonium as all the paddle adventurers have arrived early, excited for this much-anticipated day on the water. Dizzy, standing guard outside the changing rooms, but looking as if she's expecting to run inside, is back wearing her noise-cancelling headphones. She gives me a basic smile and gestures a thumbs up – maybe meaning she's OK, maybe meaning her mum's OK – but she doesn't look well. I'm glad now to have said yes to helping out.

Yesterday may have been difficult, but today will be better. It has to be.

I remember months ago Gladys told me to get to know the competition. I've no idea who Chevelle is – named on Flame's SWOT – and when it comes to Ellie, I've totally failed to get to know her. Even on this trip when she's actually working for #OutdoorSisters together with me it's going to be hard as she is paddling at the front of the group, and I'm at the back. Being so like Flame she was surely always the shoo-in candidate, if #OutdoorSisters is big enough for her ambition. This really jars, given that it might be too big for "desperate" me.

"Hi, I'm just so glad you could make it last minute," yells Ellie friendlily from the far end of the paddle shed. "And remind me I want to talk to you about the next Canal Festival." Minutes later she's marshalling the expectant group towards the pontoons. To honour the occasion and start us off she raises her fancy carbon fibre paddle towards the east, picks up her board and challenges us with a rallying cry of, "Right paddle people, who's ready to adventure?"

We all cheer, and then we're off – ten paying clients led by the effervescent Ellie. She celebrates reaching the first lock by snapping herself in a cool yoga pose. She's a moving miracle if one of her legs is artificial. It seems so unfair that a one-legged teenager (well, give or take 15 years) is both richer and better than I am as a prospective, sorry, actual, leader for a paddleboarding business. I pinch myself on my left arm in a bid to bring my nasty side under control. What will be, will be. And there's no point torturing myself as Flame didn't name the person who's won, she just said it wasn't me.

Paddling confidently we soon reach a lock. Here the group clamber off their boards and portage to the other side, knowing it's the first of 16 along our route, fresh enough to try not to let our long boards swing into the overtaking cyclists and sweating runners, who all seem determined to break their Strava records today, despite the heat warnings.

Back on the canal the exuberant Lulie, a brown-haired teacher paddling at the very back of our group laughs at the people speeding away this beautiful day, then offers to water splash the bearded runner squeezing past the crowds, barefoot shoes riskily close to the canal edge.

"How about you splash me instead," I counter, "but you better chase me to do it," and with that I paddle off a bit faster in the hope a challenge might encourage Lulie to put some welly into her paddle strokes. But even notching our slowest paddleboarder up a gear we are all really just pootling down this stretch past the Other Boat Club towards Acton's Lock at far less than 3.5 km per hour according to someone's phone app. Anyway a languid drift is alright with me, it's low effort and totally absorbing.

The towpath cyclists and runners inevitably speed past us paddle boarders – we spot Jack rattling past on a yellow fixie bike – even some walkers overtake us! I'm sure the group feels slow wins too, as we're able to enjoy seeing the teenage coots practice diving and spot little fish (minnows and roach) beneath our boards exploring sun-dappled patches of water.

After admiring the zebra-like markings on a statue-still heron fishing, Ahmed asks why there is always a dumped electric bike and a stripey bollard resting on the bottom of the canal whenever we come to a bridge. These sacrificed items are such a common occurrence you'd think it was a ritual to the water gods ordered by the cool people of Hackney Wick to keep their sourdough rising and coffee beans ground.

There's really a lot of rubbish in the canal if you pay attention when the sunlight shines. I'd rather not.

Near the abandoned gasometers Ellie pops into a headstand and we stop for a long drink. "I saw you got caught up in the guerilla Canal-ival," says Ellie passing out strawberries 'for-energy'. "It was crazy this year! I've never seen so many people or boats milling around. We were trying out a few moves for the Canal Festival show, 'cos Flame usually puts something together, and ended up being trapped at the Hoxton Docks warehouse for about three hours while the police poured water on the party," when she notices my shocked face I sense she's about to joke, "Not literally!" but of course, this is the moment that Lulie catches up with me. She whacks her paddle into the water producing a mini wave that finds its way into my unclipped dry bag soaking this morning's hastily put-together banana sandwich. I'm totally soaked too, think dripping laundry before the spinning stage, but it's already 28C degrees so more than welcome. Or would be if her tsunami hadn't also knocked my glasses off my face and into the canal.

"Glug, blah, glug glug?" says someone near my elbow.

"I'm sorry, I couldn't hear what you said," I try to reply. There's something strange about losing your glasses, it also means you can't hear what's going on. "I'm not normally deaf," I garble, taking safety on my knees. I listen to a commotion around me, a person plopping into the water and then splashes of colour as if a luminous kingfisher has dived into the canal. Suddenly an arm emerges by my nose holding my glasses. I take them, wipe them down and replace them on my head. I can hear again, and see! Lulie is super apologetic and full of detail about how Ellie came to the rescue – she's definitely got a girl crush.

Ellie at last gets the chance to check I'm OK. "I was so lucky to find your glasses, I just did a sweep on the bottom and there they were. They're OK aren't they? Not broken?" I hear myself echoing her words, "OK, not broken," but I think something is wrong, there's a definite rose-tinted hue to Ellie who has literally saved my paddling day. "They might need more cleaning," she adds, "as there's a bit of petrol on the surface here. I absolutely stink of it now after going in. The joys of urban paddling!"

"Well don't light up will you, else the canal will catch fire," joshes Lulie's friend, another big yoga with Flame fan. "Bit of a waste if there's no Viking body to burn."

We paddle on, chatting curiously about which musician is likely to open the Canal Festival in early September – past superstars have included Spandau Ballet, Leona Lewis, Alexandra Burke, Jazzie B, Little Simz and Alan Parker. "Has Alan Parker got any songs we can paddle along to," says Lulie curiously, which leads to a big debate about whether you'd spend your last cash on a gig or a Netflix subscription, though I'm wondering distractedly how Bio Queen managed to get these Islington superstars to open what's really a village fun day. She must have amazing connections for someone who never seems to have more than three customers in her tiny cafe.

It's high summer, but just as you know that autumn isn't far away there's a sense that we're reaching the end of 2,000 miles of navigable canals that link inland Britain's former industrial towns to the Limehouse. Back in the day that's where the barges would have loaded their goods on to bigger vessels for global trading. As we pass through a final lock on the Regent's Canal the tatty narrowboats with their repurposed Henry Hoovers planted up with chard, tomatoes and sunflowers and the holiday stop 'n' shop barges moored along the towpath from Angel to Victoria Park are gone, replaced by big shiny cruisers moored up and waiting to motor on to the Thames. Even the 14 foot board Ellie is using looks tiny beside these gin palaces.

Here at the Limehouse marina, one lock from the Thames, it's a beautiful day. The water sparkles, the white yachts look sleek and their flags blow and clink against the cables transporting us from our little canal to the millionaire and billionaire's land of boats, crew, uniform. "You don't have to be super-rich: my school friend from back home and her husband and baby live in that narrowboat, in the marina over there," says Lulie pointing. "We should go and visit her – I'm sure she's in because their bikes are on the roof." And we probably would have done so, if at that moment Ellie hadn't noticed 40 silhouetted Anthony Gormley like figures, though all alive and wearing cover robes, lining the marina edges. "Oh, my goodness, it's the Wild Water Women," she says, enthusiastically taking photos. "I think we're going to see their Anti Algal Bloom Boom display."

At exactly the moment the basin clock chimes midday, the pink-hatted swimmers remove their coaty-cloaks and start to climb down the marina's ladders. It's a steep drop, but when they're deep enough they launch into the water and swim out about 10m, each trailing a little pink tow float behind them. From here their swim-cap clad heads look tiny, no bigger than a moorhen chick.

"Well that's definitely taboo in the Limehouse," says Ellie knowledgeably.

Soon the swimmers fall into formation, all swimming front crawl towards the sun as they head in a shoal towards the opposite side. I'm so busy focusing on their climb back up the ladders that what's happening is confusing. Bobbing low in the water on our boards it's not easy to see, but it seems that the swimmers have managed to hook up some kind of line across Limehouse Basin because suddenly a massive campaigning banner emerges from the cold, deep water emblazoned with the words SWIMMERS SAY TIME TO CLEAN UP on it. Ellie, still smiling, captures it all on her Go Pro camera. Our little group then chats about direct action until a couple of police cars with blazing sirens arrive making it hard to hear ourselves. We do see a drone launched by the swimmers is grounded. And then the show's over, banner confiscated, and women off the water.

"Wasn't that great, bet that's all over our screens later on," says Ellie happily.

I don't wish to be churlish, but I'm not really sure what it was that I've witnessed. Interesting, yes, but it certainly wasn't what I'd call great, besides I'm not sure how 10 leisure paddleboarders witnessing it, will help publicise the swimmers' cause. I can't even remember what their confiscated banner said. But at least the action gave my aching shoulders a comfort break.

Now from the canal side comes a piercing wolf whistle. It's a long way off, but I think I can make out the figures of Jack and blonde-haired Flame. They have the sun behind them, so are more like paper cut outs, but when we see them wave, we paddle out of the main channel towards where they are standing on Commercial Lane Lock.

"Oh wow, Flame's with Jack and her puppy, isn't that the cutest creature?" says someone.

All the women paddleboarders coo, and it's true, Pericles is an adorable curly-haired pup. But the sight of a fleet of paddleboards makes him leap around enough to wriggle out of Flame's arms. We watch, shocked, as the puppy dives out of Flame's grip and plops into the lock by the side of a huge boat. Even from here I can hear Flame scream at the man just packing up his windlass. Her puppy is only 14 or 15 weeks old and can't have that much sense, and is perhaps only just discovering how to doggy paddle. But we can't stop watching – time frozen – as Jack leaps confidently from the lock side on to the narrowboat. He must say something soothing to the people at its helm, as they don't seem half as surprised as you'd expect by his invasion. We watch as Jack leans to the starboard side and makes encouraging noises to attract the puppy over so he can scoop it out of the fast-filling lock by its scruff neck. Dangling Pericles looks like a soggy pyjama case, but he's rescued, alive and well.

"As Jack would say, that was a sup-erb rescue," says Lulie generously.

Ellie has filmed all this too. She looks impressed by Jack's quick responses, almost as if she didn't think this was typical of the man she trains.

"Wow, he did well. I'm not even sure that he likes dogs much, he's more into killing animals than rescuing them," she says loud enough for most of us to hear. I'm quite shocked she's not a Jack fan, but most of the group seem unphased by this revelation. "He's a rodent exterminator not a butcher," says Lulie admitting that she booked him last Christmas before her mother-in-law came to stay and he actually removed a rat's nest. "You'd definitely fear him if you were a mouse, but I think dog or cat ought to be alright," she says in half-jest, though she's clearly not been chatting to Bio Queen about Jack's unfortunate track record with cats.

"Shall we go calmly up to them and find out if everything is OK?" suggests Ellie, bringing us all back to the current drama. There's a murmur of yes, all of us horribly aware that both Jack and the escapee pup might not have ended safely canalside. As we paddle closer we can see Flame in tears as she hugs her naughty puppy. "He's so slippery; when he wriggles he feels like quicksilver," she's sobbing. "I've no idea how I'm going to get him to stay still long enough for me to practise yoga on the board."

I think there was a moment like this in my life, perhaps every woman's life, when you realise that everything you like doing is on hold until you can figure out how to find a doppleganger. For me it was a childminder then school. For my mum it was a cleaner:

women paying women paying women in ever decreasing amounts so that they can do the things they used to do. Or like doing. Or perhaps don't like doing.

"Well Jack might be your dog walker and your successor if you ask nicely, Flame," jokes someone. She always senses a love affair where none could possibly exist.

"Is Jack going to run #OutdoorSisters?" I hear myself saying rather bitterly as the paddlers crowd around the dog. I think only Ellie notices this as she brings her board over beside mine and soothingly says, "But he can't, he's a bloke with a job and endurance race plans that takes up a lot of his time. What's more the whole point of #OutdoorSisters is that it's set up for empowering women."

I hadn't thought of that. If Ellie is right, then I now know that *she* must be the one Flame has negotiated to be the new her. I wish I didn't like her so much. It's hard to hate your winning rival if they've been nice company all day, and even more importantly rescued your glasses from the canal version of Davy Jones' locker.

16. ONLY JOKING AT THE *BUDDLEIA* NARROWBOAT CAFE

Last minute planning for the Canal Festival

Of course we end our long day's paddle at the Narrowboat Cafe. "Bio Queen would never forgive us if we didn't," says Ellie encouraging our paddlers to relax after the long trip before they return home.

Our visit doesn't start well. "I'm far too busy for customers," snaps Bio Queen discouragingly as our little group arrives, bringing an end to the chat about who took the photo that really sums up our Big One paddle. Surprised, I look around and can only see two people, USP and Martyn (the pale one), on board. Just as Lulie turns to go Ellie beams a smile at Bio Queen and waves us all on board.

"She's always hyper or mardy, just like this, in the countdown to the Canal Festival. Having a few customers will soon jolt her back to her usual self," says Ellie confidently, gesturing for me to join her at one of the starboard-side tables with a view towards the Boat Club.

I always forget how well the Boat Club crew know each other, I think they were all in the youth club, though maybe at different times, but it does mean that Gladys and Bio Queen have literally seen them grow up.

"Alright," agrees Bio Queen, surprisingly meekly as Ellie gets people settled at the less than comfy tables, "as long as one of you" – she looks directly at me – "will volunteer to wash the dishes and do a bit of deck swabbing, or as you might know it, cleaning up, then you can all have homemade vegan cheese scones and a choice of Hackney IPA, homemade hawthorn cordial or my special wine, £10 a person, plus some ideas for the upcoming Canal Festival please. Or if that doesn't suit, then just buzz off to the Co-op supermarket and get yourself some Red Bull and hummus to eat in the park. You'll thank me whatever you choose."

We stay, flopping over the trolley tables and chairs, scattering (as neatly as we can) bags of spare clothes and Tupperware boxes now filled with nothing but crumbs, banana skins and apple cores. Bio Queen, in an unexpected combo of outsize embroidered silk shirt and no jewellery, with her wild hair tucked into a tight knot on the top of her head, tuts at our mess.

As the scones heat up all the paddleboarders talk is about the Big One, the aching shoulders, the near misses, the dream of using a carbon fibre paddle, the wildlife seen and the just-in-time rescue of Flame's puppy. Meanwhile, Bio Queen busies herself behind the counter with a mountain of crockery, occasionally shouting out festival ideas as if they were a shopping list. I can see USP is taking notes so he must think it is serious. Gradually we exhaust the Big One and join this brainstorm insisting that's what's needed to make this year's Canal Festival stand out are "bunting", "a show", "dyed ducks", "the Wild Water Women and their Anti Algal Bloom Boom banner", "costumes", "online petition", "litter pick display", "circular economics".

"Cheese scones, for pity's sake let cheese scones appear soon, else I'll literally die of hunger," Lulie appeals, rubbing her aching lower back before washing a painkiller down with the last of her bottled water. "Every part of me is sore now, though I felt fine on the water."

At that moment my friend Adebola comes up the gangway. To my surprise she gives a wave towards

USP's general direction. Stiffening I shuffle over to my friend and give her a hug but as talking is out of the question, now that everyone is embroiled in last minute Canal Festival planning, I go back to my seat by Ellie. Adebola in a brightly coloured crochet cardi and Capri pants takes a seat near USP. She seems to know him well!

The phrase "Crisp packet art" floats across the room, followed in quick succession by increasingly urgent tasks "a campaign ask", "themed food – maybe a grilling", "and a name, we've got to firm up the name…"

USP puts down his pen and looks over at Bio Queen as if asking if it's OK to share. "Well we have two names for the Canal Festival 2024 so far," he says grandly, clearly forgetting that some of us were in this very room, well boat, when the name was first discussed. "What do our paddleboarders think of 'Trash-spiration'? Or the '*Wholly Shit Show*'?"

"They're both good, though two different focuses," says Ellie standing up to stretch tired muscles. "I'm so looking forward to this year's Canal Festival. I know it will be great Bio Queen, you don't need to panic because you always pull it off," she adds reassuringly, simultaneously lifting her left leg up behind her in some kind of complicated pilates move that is meant to lengthen the spine and unlock tight thigh muscles. She then does the same to her right leg.

"That's better," she says, "always good to warm down."

I stare at Ellie, unable to stop wondering how she is so flexible. Looking away through the little port-hole window, which I note has had its pretty fairy lights bizarrely replaced by a garland of flattened Tango cans, I catch sight of three Canada geese, also all standing on one leg. That's it I have to ask. "Ellie, can I ask something personal?" I say. Despite the crowd, or the fact that no one is more than about four steps away from each other, I'm determined to find out what Ellie's balance magic is. Given that I'm not confident on two legs in anything other than a parallel stance on my board, I want to know how she can cope with just one leg leading a group or working as a PT. Doesn't she ever get sore?

Suddenly Ellie starts to laugh.

She's definitely laughing at me.

I can see Bio Queen, USP and Martyn all eyeballing me. I must have over-stepped the ground rules here. Ellie is choking hysterically, tears running from both her eyes.

Oh this is very bad.

Trying to catch her breath she places her hand on my shoulder, in a sort of reassuring way. "You've been so had Lara. I didn't want to keep up the pretence but the gang thought it was funny – she gestures at Bio Queen. I need to ask you, do you know what my full name is?"

The tiny, overcrowded cabin falls silent. On the canal I swear I can hear a cormorant dive, and they must be some of the quietest birds in the world.

"Yes, Ellie. Ellie Senkruraj," I say quietly. I feel like I'm about to be banished for social misdemeanours.

"Stick it into Google and you'll see it's just a made-up name, it's Esperanto for legless, or one-legged. I changed it by deed poll myself when I was recovering from a big kayaking accident years ago. It sort of gave me power over my body when I was doing physio. But I never lost a leg, I just injured one and both work great now. So the answer to the question you haven't actually asked is yes, like you I have two legs, and how do I balance so well on a paddleboard? Well, that is 10,000 hours of practice."

And then she starts to laugh again.

"Who pranked you?" shouts USP curiously as I try not to catch anyone's eye in the cafe, especially Adebola. "I'm guessing Jack, he loves to tease. Or maybe Gladys."

"Everyone really," I say truthfully after a bit of thought, though it was definitely Gladys who got the idea lodged in my brain, and she did it right where I'm sitting now.

"Anyway, no hard feelings," says Ellie when she's able to breathe again. "I should apologise really for letting you be led along."

"It gave us all something to look forward to though, the big reveal," says Bio Queen as she finally brings out plates generously piled with warm, cheesy scones. Now the *Buddleia* Narrowboat Cafe is filled with heavenly smells and the sound of bottle tops pinged off. For those decanting into a glass that nose-twitching cordial fizz when carbon dioxide bubbles meet the air. If it comes with food and friends maybe being had isn't so bad. It's definitely good for Bio Queen's morale, she's calmed down completely and is humming away.

"What happened when the air conditioning in the cheese factory broke down?" asks Lulie good naturedly, mouth full of scone, trying to inject some cheesy group humour back to the gathering. She's clearly noticed that I'm a bit shaken by being the butt of the joke. Gratefully, even I try shouting out ideas – this narrowboat cafe is the best place to get people interacting – until we eventually agree that 'meltdown' is the best of the answers. I wouldn't advise Lulie to quit her day job and start writing cracker jokes.

Note to self, never agree to help Bio Queen, however persuasive, and even if she's willing to serve up food masquerading as nectar of the Gods after a day-long paddle. The next hour sees me washing dishes and sprucing the *Buddleia's* deck. Adebola and USP help me until she pleads a headache intense enough for her to need to get home, so I never manage to talk to her about Greg's exit. I do find out how my friend knows USP though, turns out it was at one of Flame's land-based yoga socials. I should go to one...

As I scrub on I begin to think just how much cleaners like Gladys have to put up with, but nowhere more than those working around boats which have to look good whatever the weather, have everything on show (because there's no storage), and if converted into a cafe must also be Health, Hygiene and Hurricane safe.

After all the dishwashing and then shunting the empties down to the nearest recycling bottle bank (a ten minute walk each way), Bio Queen puts me on duty polishing the foredeck's three metre brass rail. This is followed by a challenge to make her hollow rubber doormat squeaky clean, a task that requires an electric toothbrush. And floss.

After Adebola goes, USP is half-chatting to Bio Queen about planned episodes of the *Wholly Shit Show*, and unless it's my imagination, half-flirting with me. As he goes to leave – back to the studio apparently – he pats me on the hair (definitely over-friendly) and says cryptically, "Now you know why the British Navy was obliged to trick youngsters into service."

Baffling, especially when he then did a two finger salute (like guns to the temple), before slouching on to the gangplank to light a cigarette and head back to his podcast world. At least he didn't quote Hegel at me again.

17. LET'S GET THIS FESTIVAL STARTED

Flame has a job for Lara

Most Sundays the early morning sessions at the Boat Club are extraordinarily peaceful – you can hear the waterfowl gossiping, and with the late summer wind blowing south westerly the traffic noise on City Road doesn't disturb this nature bubble. I love admiring the plants growing in the battered old green canoe by the entrance, and along one of the less busy pontoons the dagger spears of purple loosestrife are buzzing with bees. As the sun heats up the big old terrapin scrabbles on to one of the tyre fenders of the permanently moored barge office, *Deep Water,* and then, boom, it's time for the bell to start buzzing as staff and kids arrive. Water peace replaced with something just as good, a hive of outdoor splash and learn beneath Islington's tallest tower blocks.

But today it's the first Sunday in September and the once-a-year Canal Festival, so peace isn't on the agenda. Even when I struggle along at 7am, two strong black coffees short of bright-eyed wakefulness, the nearest streets and the towpath are heaving with volunteers in high-vis tabards setting up for the borough's big end of summer get-together.

"There are just so many helpers," I shout approvingly towards Flame when I reach our rendezvous point – the *Buddleia* Narrowboat Cafe. "Absolutely," she says without really listening. "Now could you take on sup pup duties for the next couple of hours? I know it's not paddleboarding, but you're the most reliable person I know round here today." Flame then hands me the lead of her waggy-tailed puppy and a bag packed with doggy kit. Pericles jumps up and licks my mouth. It feels like approval that first time. But from then on every time I try to look at the typed itinerary of what he needs, sit down or move, his paws are on my shoulder and his tongue is licking my mouth.

"Oh he's kissing you. How sweet!" says Flame at the same time as I'm thinking this dog's tongue is a seriously gross health hazard. Her total misjudgement stops me from protesting at either the dog's behaviour or her request, because if I'd had time to think, I'd definitely have said no. On the plus side at least I've upgraded from doormat to dog walker.

"Obviously I'm paying you for your time," she adds, just in case I am creative enough to think of an excuse.

"You can't seriously be leaving that teething monster with Lara are you?" asks a voice. Yet again USP has turned up unexpectedly where Flame seems to be. Flame laughs good naturedly, always less surprised to see him than I am. "Well I did ask you Simon, but I seem to remember you turned down the honour to focus on your live show."

With dog on string (in fact a rather fancy padded harness and leather lead, plus instructions to apply sun cream on the pale bits of this pampered pooch's muzzle, on the hour), I pick up one of the hireable deck chairs (nice touch festival organisers) and sit myself in the shade of the *Buddleia* Narrowboat Cafe. There's not much chance of invisibly people-watching if you're with a puppy as cute as Pericles with his soft blonde curls and endless happiness. The less busy setter-uppers and as time ticks on to the opening, the first festival goers, keep stopping to ask the pup's name, age and breed. Every one of them gets a mouth lick. I read in Flame's notes that this is something I'm not meant to encourage, but I have no idea how to stop it.

"Have you figured out why he kisses everyone? Or indeed, what dogs are so happy about yet?" asks USP, coming to sit by me while he has a cigarette. Despite the growing heat he's in his usual black polo neck plus dark jeans. Admittedly he has added an oversize straw hat to provide a bit of shade, perhaps because he heard the weather warnings that this would be the hottest September day ever, with air quality compromises and risk of heat stroke for some. Listening to the weather report when I woke up, I did wonder if the weather guys realise quite how much Londoners love the sun. If they want us to stay indoors or alter our behaviour as the climate changes they might try using a report from a cold, grey February day rather than getting upset about a sunny summer.

"No idea with Pericles, he's permanently smiling," I eventually say trying to look nonchalant by adding a semi-Gallic shrug, only to find my shoulders are still tight from that long paddle to Limehouse.

"I'm doing a live podcast – well radio type thing – during the festival. I don't suppose you'd be willing to help out a bit?" asks USP confidently. "I'm doing the recording at about 11am, so you'd need to get over to the studio 'boat' ten minutes or so before, without the dog."

"I don't think I can compromise about the dog, so he'll have to come if you want me," I say thinking I've definitely escaped the horror of doing another podcast. Apparently this is not an acceptable get out clause as USP laughs, and says, "Fine, see you both later, and have fun 'til then."

He stalks away blowing mock air kisses at Pericles (or me). He really is a very strange man.

As the clock counts down to the grand opening with four big hitters – the Mayor, a local MP, an ancient *Eastenders* villain and a fabulously made-up influencer – everyone in a high vis vest is urging everyone else to, "Have a great festival!" Apart from buying slabs of cake and staring at the water (which I'd rather be on) there isn't much to do when you are in charge of a hot dog.

"Sup-lady, if I said 'how cute' you'd know I was talking about the dog, wouldn't you?" says Jack, friendly to Pericles as he passes. He's wearing an unusually brown set of clothes, shorts and shirt, though you can't see much of him because he's carrying a huge paddleboard under each arm.

"Were you there when the daft show name was dreamt up? We've been having such fun with the scatological title," he says conversationally. "Even Bio Queen is unable to sup-press her mirth. Anyway I think you'll enjoy the sup-rise Lara, even if you saw a bit of it a few weeks ago at the crazy Canal-ival… Just keep an eye on the water won't you?" Before I can quiz him, he's gone, heading towards the *Buddleia* Narrowboat Cafe.

When Pericles starts to whine I take his hint and go for a slow stroll. Turns out that all the roads around City Road Lock, from the little stone bridge up to the pub and the main high street are closed. It's still quite early but there are hundreds of people wandering around. I spot a couple of paddling clients browsing the stalls, and follow them discreetly only to overhear them joking about very on message topics including having a narrowboat holiday, saving up for a helmsman course, their hopes of winning the raffle (two hours for six friends in a hot jacuzzi tug with ample prosecco at Canary Wharf) before buying a large meadow sweet from the herb stall that specialises in 'plants for your own garden pond'.

"Not sure we'll manage to get our deposit back if we dig a pond in the crappy third floor flat we're renting," giggles one. "But doesn't this plant smell good?" Private detectives must need a high boredom threshold.

Triggered by the word "smells" I begin to realise just how many stalls are selling fancy street food – and how hungry I'm starting to feel without breakfast. The whole festival seems to be a massive excuse to eat delicious things outside. Pericles' nose is now working overtime as he scouts crumbs, dropped bamboo cutlery, little sauce pots, sticky chicken wing bones and a myriad of other dog-tasty or sniffable goodies. He crunches his finds up noisily, refusing my increasingly frantic suggestions of 'leave' and 'drop' to abandon his unexpected treasures.

At the next stall I buy a jackfruit and kimchi burger which I slowly eat while also feasting my eyes on the action. I've been to the Canal Festival before – it's like a giant fete – but I've never really noticed how many other local people are also drawn to this end of summer water celebration.

The steadily growing crowd flows past the Old Lock pub into Graham Street Park and then back along a specially created floating walkway to the City Road Lock. Here Pericles produces a giant poo mid path. Rummaging through his backpack I can't seem to find any of the biodegradable poop bags Flame provided, so I crouch down and do my best to steer his steaming turd into an old takeaway coffee cup that's been dropped by a bench. Litter has its uses today. In contrast to the lovely food smells, the dog's poo stinks, so I snap a carelessly discarded lid as tightly as I can on top. As a precaution I then wedge the cup upright into the bag, but get distracted when Ahmed the paddler bumps into me.

"Hello Lara. Are you a dog lover like Flame?"

"Absolutely not!" I say unable to stop Pericles jump up at Ahmed for a licky greeting. "Anyway this isn't a real dog, he's an AI puppy." Ahmed backs away as Pericles sets his sights for more kisses, but good humouredly chuckles. "Well that's lucky because I don't like dogs either."

I apologise, horribly aware of this dog's bad manners and the terrible stink from my bag (well Pericles' backpack). I bend to sort everything out, trying to push the stinking cup securely down a layer when through the legs of the crowd I can see something exciting is happening on the water. Remembering Jack's tip off I gingerly edge myself to the towpath and spot Flame and all of the original #OutdoorSisters contenders, except me, in action.

So that's why I'm holding Flame's bloody dog I think, rather forgetting my lack of SUP skills.

Flame is back on the aerial hoop, this time it's attached to a heavily-branded Canal & River Trust gantry and crane brought in to erect a floating pontoon stage in the centre of the basin. And on this stage, beneath Flame's expansive toe points and arm swings, Ellie is doing a full yoga show. It's exactly the routine they were trialling on the day of the crazy Canal-ival. From here I can see that Jack is in charge of the music. OK, this all makes sense – perhaps they were practising the other day. But then the music starts to jazz up, builds into a crescendo and suddenly a woman in a skin-tight yellow top and leggings runs across the stage and leaps off – but instead of splash landing in the canal, like everyone else would, she plops perfectly in the centre of a paddleboard, and starts to do tricks that no human should be able to manage. She's wearing her headphones, presumably to make the show look a bit crazier for the audience, and looks to me very recognisably like Dizzy. Except she's amazing at SUP – jumping from centre to back of the board, whizzing it around 360 degrees (the famous step back turn), then leaping to the front and doing the same move but this time the board's fins are right out of the water as they skim a perfect circle.

I'm not sure how much skill the audience realises this move needs – most seem to think it's a miracle to just balance on a board and paddle with the wind behind you. But my mouth opens so wide in a gasp of admiration that Pericles takes advantage, leaps up and gives me a wet slobber. I step abruptly away from his dog breath grimacing, trip and fall spread-eagled into a nasty green patch of water. Because I don't let go of his lead the poor dog is dragged in too, landing on to my shoulder and pushing me properly under.

Don't panic. Make a star shape. Find the surface. Surely in a canal with an average depth of 1.3 metres and in sight of this massive crowd I really shouldn't be drowning… Someone will save us…

Me and the dog are arms and paws crashing around in the soupy water, making such a commotion that gallant Dizzy, despite needing to interrupt her mid-spinning performance, paddles over and hoists us both out in the most dramatic of rescues, board flipped over and with a 3-2-1 crosses my arms, grabs my hands, and even though I'm still holding Pericles' lead, she lifts. To the crowd it must look totally staged, a star recovering a nearly drowned woman and dog, but when Dizzy sees that it's me she's pulled up she just starts to laugh and laugh. The crowd laughs along, clapping and cheering.

Now I know that we're both safe, it's actually quite a relief to have had this cooling off moment. I'm sure Pericles thinks so too.

Accompanied by the booma boom beat and the crowd's claps Dizzy lightning paddles us towards today's impromptu floating stage. Here Jack helps me disembark and then points to a spot by his feet where me and the dog can dry out in the sun. I slink to the floor but cheer up slightly when from the hoop Flame throws me an air kiss. And then the performing trio of SUP women get back to the show – utter professionals.

The show's interrupted again – this time intentionally – by a couple, both wearing red boiler suits, who start to hang up homemade bunting. It looks as if Bio Queen has had a hand in this as that's definitely not your traditional fluttering pinks, mauves and light green triangles seen at bank holiday get-togethers, instead the bunting makes a sort of crunching sound as the lunchtime breeze catches it. Ah, I get it, this is crisp packet art by Frida and the pale zombie, Martyn, the perfect collaboration to kick start the Trashspiration Canal Festival.

Ellie and Flame pass the stage over to the next act, the Wholly Shit mime artists who I can just about recognise from our litter pick. From my corner of the pontoon they seem to be taking us on a paddle down the canal while finding all sorts of strange objects – a woman rides a Lime bike across the stage. She's followed by a bloke with a bollard on his head which gets anyone who loves Glasgow, Scotland, or bollards, clapping. More crisp bunting is wrapped around the floating stage and once hung the performers mimic plogging – jogging a few metres, then stopping to synchronise the movement of a litter picking arm snapping open and shut, rather like something you'd see in a contemporary ballet at Sadler's Wells.

The mime artists are building to a crescendo (well the music is) as a suitcase is discovered, then unpacked and inside we have a gun, no two guns; a UC form, a body.

Yes, I suppose all these rather random things have been discovered in the canal given that it began to be dug before the Battle of Waterloo, but on my litter picks it's more often scraps of ice cream wrappers, sandwich packaging, aluminium cans and hot drink cups – boring stuff.

In the hot sun of the pontoon I drift into a reverie about the need to create a long, long list of the implicated brands and then taking their CEOs for a paddleboard which ends with them having their portraits taken up-close alongside soggy branded litter from their companies. We could have a chat about the pointlessness of putting litter, even fished-out litter into the temporary storage of another rubbish bin, and how this has simply tidied something unpleasant up that's going to soon end up in landfill. I can see myself telling the CEOs how this doesn't solve the problem of their bright litter messing up the canal. "Because if you had, #OutdoorSisters wouldn't be running so many litter picks all season, despite the stink and the risk of Weil's disease and belly run." Actually they are welcome to join us. Or sponsor us.

"Hey, wake up – I think the sun's gone to your head! Impressive entry to the show, but you need to get off the stage now," says a kayaker tapping firmly on my leg. It's Jack, now in a boat. He seems to be a bit of a water pixie today, everywhere and nowhere. He gestures at the paddleboard he's towing and then hands me a buoyancy aid and paddle. I'm a bit worried that I'm expected to perform the next set of tricks, because I'm nowhere as good as Dizzy, but Jack explains it's the exact opposite, he's just got a message saying it's time for me to get off the stage and go to USP's festival studio to take one for the #OutdoorSisters team.

I can feel myself blush with happiness. They needed me in the end, I'm not just a dog sitter.

"I know it's a sup-rising request Lara, so don't go to Old Street, just get on to the towpath and look for USP's *Wholly Shit Show* flag," says Jack deadpan. He then gives Pericles a friendly pat before shoving our paddleboard in the right direction.

With the aid of a few doggy treats I manage to keep Pericles on top of the board as I paddle back across the water. I hope Flame, still up on her hoop, is impressed by my dog whispering skills. And if she is, is it too late for her to change her mind about me as her business successor? At the towpath I tie up the board to the stern of a narrowboat, wriggle up and out with Pericles tucked under one arm, paddle under the other, to go on the hunt for USP. What I don't do is plan anything to say – whatever I'm asked will have to be off the cuff.

No different from the last podcast then.

18. TRASHSPIRATION

Lara the litter champion

USP is clearly enjoying being watched by the crowds as he records in his makeshift studio – though I'm not sure who he thinks he is broadcasting to given the competing activities on offer at this Festival, as well as the pleasures of chatting to neighbours while enjoying hot weather by the canal.

He might think it's a studio, but I just see someone sitting in a biggish row boat, a bit smaller than the one Shackleton used to cross the freezing Southern Ocean, whose brought all the podcast mod cons, including headphones and mic. As I gingerly step down into the boat holding a panting Pericles, over the sound system I can hear USP's voice oddly amplified thanking his last guest. In the boat studio I have no choice but to sit so close that I know what he had for breakfast (latte and toast followed by toothpaste). He makes me feel uncomfortable, though it might be that I'm still unsure what I should be talking about. Isn't there a rule of three, where you tell the radio star what you want to say, then tell them what it is, then tell them what you told them? Or is that only possible if you are media trained, with an actual cause? I'm sure he's only asked me on air because the rest of #OutdoorSisters were planning to entertain the crowds – so it was either a sympathy ticket or expediency if no one else said yes.

As USP's voice booms across the water I pick up a festival programme and start to fan Flame's hot puppy. His ears flick – he's clearly appreciating the breeze – but spellbound by Pericles I manage to miss the clever trick that someone, presumably Bio Queen's team, has pulled off by projecting two contrasting mirages over the canal. Blink and it's so clean you can see the big fish grazing, flicking their tails in and out of water lilies: a swimmer's dream. Look away and suddenly it's a stink of sewage full of everything you've ever imagined might go into a dustcart and cesspit but topped by dead ducks caught up in carelessly discarded fishing wire and yesterday's picnic.

It's got the crowd's attention though.

"Hello, hello Trashspiration Canal Festival! Now we have Lara Lake, a great friend of the canal and a fabulously keen litter picker. What do you think of the *Wholly Shit Show* so far?" he says efficiently, big smile, eyes unnervingly locked on mine as he passes over a headset.

"Um, yes, thank you for inviting me today. And yes, so far it's been a really good day on and off the water," (although as I say that I realise I'm not sure who realises that I've also been *in* the water today too).

"The Canal Festival is always the best event and look at the turnout, it's great," I say nervously glancing at the crowds milling around the narrowboats. That's when I see that along the towpath most people are now staring at the water in disbelief as the life-affirming, then sewage-despairing, holograms keep flashing up. You'd think I had cold water shock the way my breath is husking all over the place, but slowly I calm myself down and start to spot friends: Jack's chatting to Dizzy away to my left and there are some old neighbours. And now here come's Gladys, who I haven't seen for ages. Everyone is here today!

"Yes, let's give ourselves and the Trashspiration Canal Festival organisers the cheer they deserve," says USP, who seems very used to building up a crowd. He pauses and I think I can hear some excited shouts from the towpath. Perhaps this is a live broadcast. Strange to think of this wooden boat's occupants' conversation catching the attention of these big crowds. When I later watch videoed snippets I can see this nice/nasty transformation of the canal compels people to stop their chatter and listen to the booming broadcast as if we had the answers.

"So back to litter picking. Now I hear that you do this from the paddleboards at #OutdoorSisters. Is it easy? Can anyone join?" asks USP.

I try to explain that you have to pay to litter pick, so no. But also that anyone can pick up litter, anytime, so yes. And if people walking or lunching by the towpath stopped dropping litter, then no one would have to pay and we could just paddle gently up and down the canal admiring ragged robin flowers, mallard ducks, dragonflies and bats rather than vying with each other to spot the most litter created by Nestle, Unilever and many other big brands.

"So as Hegel would say, 'Evil resides in the very gaze which perceives Evil all around itself,'" says USP impenetrably.

"Well, maybe, I don't really understand what that means," I stutter, heading off on a garbled tangent as if I've forgotten this is live on air. "I kind of like your intellectual quips, but whenever you say 'Hegel' I just hear, 'Hey gal' and then I think of those seagulls 'Hey gull, get it?" using the really tall Canaletto building as a cliff edge they can swoop down from and pick off the baby coots, or whatever a baby coot is called, a cootlet?"

USP sticks to his point.

"Well Lara, as this is the *Wholly Shit Show* I think we should talk about how the water companies are actually allowed to discharge untreated sewage full of E.coli bacteria – from raw poo in case you didn't realise – into rivers and lakes and the sea when there are big rainstorms. What's more they don't have to pay to do this or tell anyone, they just do it, flushing sewage into rivers and of course that's going to mean some leakage into this canal too. For example in just one year, 2021, Thames Water, which operates around here and is the UK's largest water company, released streams of raw sewage for 163,000 hours. That's like flushing the most revolting of toilets into the canal 24 hours a day for two years!"

I'm not sure I'd realised that, but I can't speak as the puppy is starting to fuss, pulling at his harness in a bid to escape. I put my hand into the bag of doggy goodies to look for a distracting treat.

USP continues: "You paddleboarders seem to spend a lot of time picking up litter, which you say the people here right now, the people who walk along by the canal are actually responsible for – aren't you focusing on the wrong things?"

"Wow, that's rude," I snap, forgetting I'm talking publicly on air, simultaneously grabbing at a soft-feeling treat which I keep closed in my hand – a nice smell to distract the pup. But as I can't escape from USP's boat studio very easily, I attack back, months of litter picking discontent released.

"It's not just big business that gets it wrong. There's no one at this festival who isn't guilty of messing up the very place we really love, our planet. Just taking this canal as an example, even if I only create one piece of litter once a year – let's say an ice cream wrapper bought because it's cheap and I'm hot, which then manages to fly out of my hand when I'm ferreting around for a phone to take a picture. There are 200,000 people living in this borough, and many more who visit, that means there could be at the minimum 200,000 bits of litter dropped totally accidentally in just one year all released by people who might not even know they've done it. Worse, even though a lot of this packaging is plastic, most of it isn't recyclable or reusable so that's 200,000 plastic ice cream wrappers to be thrown away. The point I like to make when we're mid canal is that you can't throw *anything* away, not properly I mean. You can only put rubbish into a bin, where it's moved by refuse collectors to be put into landfill either here in the UK or elsewhere. And then it sits in that big rubbish tip for years polluting the environment. So it's all of our faults, we can't just blame water companies."

"Thanks to Lara for making everyone feel bad at their once a year Canal Festival!" says USP, more friendly now. "What I'm trying to point out is that your approach is too personal. You think picking up litter (or not dropping it) makes you a good person, but as Hegel would have told you, and I'll say it again because it's such a good phrase, 'Evil resides in the very gaze which perceives Evil all around itself.' In other words, you're blaming individuals, but it's a far bigger structural problem than making a personal choice to be good or a bit careless," says USP authoritatively. "And anyway you're just fussing about litter which is not nearly such a wicked problem as sewage pollution. Sewage is terrible for the wildlife, makes us ill, pushes up water bills and has a clear and distinct source."

I look him directly in the eye, which is quite hard as the sun's forcing me to squint. "This isn't some Soviet satellite state," I say astonished by his reasoning. "We're in Islington where we do all have personal choice, it's not a 'nice to have'. So that's why I am happy to take out people on paddleboards to collect litter from the canal. And I bet the ducks, fish and insects are pleased with it too. So if anyone at today's Canal Festival wants to come along to #OutdoorSisters to help tackle this litter problem then you are very welcome – just send us a message on Instagram."

"That's another nice call for better care of our borough's blue and green spaces," says USP rather patronisingly. He seems to be wrapping up our chat in a much more comforting tone.

"And what happens when you fall in?" he persists.

"Well most people don't, and when they do they usually have their mouth shut. But if you fell in I'd say drink a Coke – the citric acid and sugar in it will kill off any dodgy bacteria," I respond, thinking how that didn't help Dizzy much the other day. Maybe she didn't drink a full can.

"Well, a big thanks to Lara the litter champion. Now we're taking a quick break, but we'll be back soon. Until then have a great time at the Canal Festival and enjoy this music from Little Simz, one of Islington's girl stars," finishes USP switching off our mics. I wait for the panel to indicate red before challenging him.

"That was pretty tough," I say giving Pericles an anxious pat – the puppy's tongue is sticking out of the corner of his mouth and he looks hot and sleepy.

"Yeah, yeah, you did well. Held it together and made people think you were nice, though you could have put in a bit more #OutdoorSisters branding. Still that's pretty tough to do!" says USP, who I note is wearing a buoyancy aid. That's a change from our first meeting.

I look away as he fans himself with a festival programme but not before I see a bead of sweat above his eyebrows. It's midday and the thermometer is flying up, just like the weather reports warned. "Wow, it's so hot," says USP. "Let's have a no litter snack to recover – I'll buy you an ice cream in a cone so there's no danger of any wrapping blowing off into the canal." He titters, as if quoting me, and then unpeels himself from the boat's wooden seat, making it tip towards the towpath wall where it's tied. That unbalances me so I shoot my arm out towards the rowlocks. Nobly USP catches hold of my hand to steady me and pretty instantly lets out a shocked gasp. "What the heck is in your hand Lara?"

The soft brown goo and sudden unpleasant stink provides us both with an answer. It's not a dog treat, that's obvious now. In shock I pull my dog-poo smeared hand away abruptly, but that makes Pericles start. The pup jumps up revitalised just by the thought of moving and with his second lunge manages to push us all overboard.

I splutter up from the murky water a bat's squeak too close for comfort to USP, but congratulate myself because I know he's got the buoyancy aid and if I grab it or, the boat, I'll be totally safe. Both of us may be covered with a light spray of green water weed but that's not going to stop me from accepting a free ice cream. "OK," I say, "I'd like an ice cream, but I think the dog's holding you to ransom for one too."

.

19. WHOLLY SHIT SHOW

USP on the spot

"I didn't expect you to do so well Lara," says USP as if we're sitting in the *Buddleia* Narrowboat Cafe rather than spluttering out mouthfuls of green weed and immersed in the canal. Falling in by the tied up boats where all the dead birds and trash gets stuck until it's hidden by fast-growing duckweed and invading floating pennywort is I'm sure a guarantee for belly troubles. I must ask Dizzy when I next see her. USP seems unconcerned by messed-up water; he's just chatting nonsense at me.

"As Hegel did in fact say, 'To be independent of public opinion is the first formal condition of achieving anything great'."

I wonder what he means, despite all his dire warnings about the state of our canal he hardly seems to notice about being semi-submerged. Just as I'm thinking he must be a water sign, probably Pisces, he kisses me right on the lips.

"I definitely couldn't see that coming," I stutter, trying to doggy paddle away from him and towards the boat just in case he felt his smacker of a kiss was a warm up to a smooch. "I can't remember when I was last kissed," I add, shocked.

"Well actually I was getting jealous of the dog, I can't see why Pericles is the only one to taste your lips," says USP moving towards me again.

I meant a human kiss of course, and do my best to shove him away as this is awkward, and definitely non-hygienic. "This is weird," I say slowly, perhaps not the clearest of 'No's', but this is not a normal situation, even for a paddleboard teacher used to falling into water. USP takes my lack of clarity as permission and with one hand now on the studio boat to steady himself, pushes towards me for another kiss in a way that makes me struggle to keep my head above water.

Pericles starts to bark as I splash in panic.

"Do you want some help extricating yourself, because the view from up here doesn't look too great?" asks someone from the bank.

"Adebola!" say me and USP together. "What are you doing?"

It's odd how my friend keeps turning up after a summer of failing to meet, but I'm so relieved another woman's here that I don't notice any edge to her voice. USP does though and gives a watery wave.

"Adebola, we need a bit of help getting out of this, could you do the honours?" he says.

My friend, gorgeous in a bright pink sun dress laughs bitterly. "You're telling me you are going to need my help getting out of this – isn't that what Mr 'I accidentally kissed a woman because we fell in the water' is supposed to want? It's pathetic. And pathetically Freudian," says Adebola speaking very fast. She looks as if she's torn between walking away and hitting me, or USP, with her chic (at any rate new to me) leather bag.

"Are you two going out?" I eventually say after clocking that her bag has USP's canal festival podcast logo on it, 'the *Wholly Shit Show*', and recalling how she had appeared as if from nowhere the other day at Bio Queen's cafe.

"Yes," snaps Adebola, "we're engaged." She holds out her left hand and there really is a ring on it. "Wow, that's beautiful," I respond automatically because that's what any friend is hardwired to say when you see blood diamonds.

"If you could just shut up Lara, something I've been suggesting you do for a long time, I'd like to find out what Simon's story is," says Adebola rudely.

"That's what I wanted to tell you," replies USP shifting into his pretend French intellectual persona, which perhaps Adebola likes as I can feel some tension shift a little. "But also I was thinking how well you illustrate Hegel's main point about self and otherness – the primordial human experience of the world. You desire me and the water, and perhaps even your friend Lara, but spend so much time estranged from them."

"Well you can tell Hegel and his idealistic mates that he should learn to keep his dick in his trousers," she snorts.

Despite all these surprises – perhaps I don't know her as well as I thought and the fact that USP the man is definitely 15 years or more younger than Adebola and me but still hasn't figured out consent – I do agree with the general point. He's just your classic bloke masquerading as an opportunist feminist.

"Understood," says USP contritely looking up at Adebola, "If I say sorry, and mean it, do you think you can help me get out of here?"

"And Lara, she needs help too," says a familiar voice from the bank. I look through a curtain of green slime and detect Dizzy, still in her bright paddleboard show gear. She holds out a long paddle towards me which I gratefully use to drag myself and the dog towards the canalside path – that reach rescue really works. She then heaves us both out, laughing as Pericles does a huge shake of water, re-soaking everyone.

Dizzy then pulls a mini bottle of antibacterial hand wash from her Palm buoyancy aid and offers me a blob. USP, who's also managed to get himself back on to the towpath, is pointedly given a double blob.

"I was watching from the *Buddleia* Narrowboat Cafe and thought I'd join in the USP hate club," says Dizzy to me and Adebola. "He's given me big financial help, so I'm in his debt now, but I can never forget that he was a bully to me when I was a kid at the Boat Club and I need you all to know about it. He called me names. That's why no one really uses my proper name anymore. 'Dizzy' was just to make sure I sounded unthreatening, someone the boys in the kayaks would be easily able to beat."

"Look Dizzy, or Chevelle if you prefer, I am genuinely sorry," interrupts USP. "I've tried to talk to you about this in the past, all this summer, and I'd like to do it again now. I was stupid and I picked on you. You know how pissed off Flame was with me when she found out. But in my defence, I was a teenage boy who made a mistake... I know you think I was racist, but, well, I was just a bully, which is bad too, I get that, and I am trying to make up for it."

Adebola and Dizzy both square their shoulders.

"You were at university then and I was a child in a youth club," says Dizzy fiercely. I'm so hooked by this reveal that I stop trying to figure out everyone's precise ages. To be fair I've not really been able to age people since I turned 40. Maybe that's what's happened to USP?

Dizzy who never really spoke much, is as articulate as anyone I've ever heard despite the sun's heat, the situation and the horrible memories.

She stares USP in the eyes and makes sure we can all hear: "Bullying is crap, racist bullying is the worst to live through. I've always known there were haters, Mami warned me as early as she could, but I didn't expect the haters to be pretending to be a friend, and willing to manipulate everyone so it looked like I was the weak link. You lost me my place in the kayak team for the London Youth Games. Your behaviour meant I stopped paddling for years. That will always suck."

"I'm so sorry Chevelle, honestly," responds USP. "And I have tried to make it up to you. And as you know, I'm still trying."

Dizzy nods, possibly accepting this apology, and turns towards me. "Come on Lara. We need to get Pericles back to Flame so you can help me run some paddleboarding tasters after the speeches." With that she stalks off towards the *Buddleia* Narrowboat Cafe.

I follow, damply.

20 CRISIS AT THE *BUDDLEIA* NARROWBOAT CAFE

Home truths for Lara

It's the most crowded I've ever seen the *Buddleia* Narrowboat Cafe, but as Dizzy walks up the gangplank, me and the dog following, people stop talking. "You were amazing," says Bio Queen to Dizzy while the Mayor diplomatically agrees the paddle tricks were impressive.

"You've been such a super star today and we're all really pleased you're the new Flame too," says Bio Queen handing Dizzy an elderflower cordial.

As I look around for Flame – I really have to hand this dog back – I can see that Bio Queen has encouraged her staff and acolytes to make their own shit costumes. "It's all ideas borrowed from Surfers Against Sewage," she says loudly addressing the rather puzzled looking Mayor who is in a wheelchair and on duty, so unable to escape the seven feet high tubular poos gathering around her by the *Buddleia* Narrowboat Cafe gang plank. "We've even got one to escort you for the rest of the festival, our little gift from canal lovers to canal lovers," she says with a generous smile introducing Turd 2 as if they were a unique handmade gift.

"So, when did the Canal Festival become themed?" asks the Mayor stoically, though a close observer would notice that one hand is fidgeting with her heavy chain of office, even if the other is regally waving at poos. It's lucky she's had practice being out celebrity-ed by giant costume-clad creations like the Arsenal dinosaur on many Mayoral walkabouts. As her predecessor advised, when it's getting farcical or difficult, just keep smiling.

"Well, if I'm honest, I'm not sure that it has become themed," says Bio Queen dishonestly. It's almost as if she's the Mayor's doppelgänger, adopting her polite vocabulary and costume – she's today dressed all in red and dangling almost the same weight of gold medallions around her neck as the Mayor's office chains. "We've been running this cafe for enough years to see how the water quality has deteriorated and litter has piled up at the same time as the canal's become a more and more important green space for unwinding and getting up close to nature. My friend Flame who runs the paddleboard business – you probably watched her group doing their amazing *Wholly Shit Show* – calls this bit of the canal our 'blue space', rather than green space, and says it's as important for the ecosystem, you know, birds and bees that stuff, as it is for relaxing the minds of people who visit or live here. We all really need to appreciate this blue space more, don't you think?"

The Mayor, smiling widely, lets Bio Queen chat on. The local press photographer plops their body in front of mine so she can focus tightly on the three women in red – Bio Queen, Mayor and Dizzy – all dwarfed by Turd 2. Soon everyone packed into the cafe starts to clap as they recognise Dizzy as the star SUP performer who rescued the 'drowning' woman and dog.

Dizzy looks a bit bemused by the attention and of course USP, who in a space of minutes seems to have forgotten the recent fracas and lost Adebola, asks if she'll go on his show later. To my surprise she agrees.

He then turns to me and says: "Can I ask you a question?" in that mocking tone of his, definitely echoing what I'd said to Ellie at this exact spot when we were planning for this event.

"If it's anything to do with going on your podcast again then the answer's definitely no," I say rather snappily. I'm just so cross that I never guessed Dizzy was the new Flame. I mean I like her, but it doesn't make any sense. Her name wasn't even on Flame's list. Or was it? Dizzy's 'Chevelle' and the 'Other One' then. I'm more sleepwalker than paddleboarder.

USP looks a bit put out by my response as he's used to me being a pushover. I'm sure he'll have no trouble finding other guests.

Gladys, looking like herself again in wide-legged linen trousers and a strappy top, finishes the last of a green tea then turns to me with a grin. "You know, I don't think that was the question that man wanted to ask." Rudely, I ignore her too – my head is so messed up. At that moment Pericles senses Flame entering the cafe and drags me towards her.

"I just don't know what's going on," I say helplessly to Flame as Pericles leaps and bounces with delight. "This whole contest has been so stressful and yet everyone else looks a million dollars on it. Did I misunderstand about us all being offered a fair chance to take over your business?"

"I'm so sorry you feel this way Lara," she says, "and thank you a million times for looking after my furry boy this morning. Once the festival is over let's have a coffee and really talk it through."

It's a kind offer, but I'm not sure I'm interested in hearing my mistakes and failures itemised.

"Oh, look it's Gladys, looking great again, let's find out how she is," says Flame, tactfully changing conversational direction. "You know she's been very ill don't you?"

Um, no I did not. "I just thought Dizzy was doing more of her work. What happened?"

"Well let's go and ask, I'm sure she'll be able to explain better – but I might just have to take Pericles out of this crowd. Go on, go chat to her," insists Flame being steered out of the cafe and down the gangplank by her dog.

"I think you said you don't know what's going on," said Gladys. "I keep overhearing your conversations with Flame's brother and thought I might give you some wise advice."

"Wait!" I say meaning to talk about how she's been feeling, but this is astonishing, "USP is Flame's brother? But he's so old compared to her. I mean late 30 something rather than 20 something..." I try and look as if I hadn't actually been trying to precisely pinpoint his age. Can the Adebola who I knew really be going out with a toyboy? She used to be so set on only dating older men.

"Yes, we all wondered why you didn't know. If it makes it easier to follow, he's her half-brother, but they're definitely siblings, there's about 10 years between them," says Gladys authoritatively sitting down with a sigh on one of the adapted shopping trolleys rescued from the canal and renamed as chairs. "I'm not sure that Bio Queen has quite got the hang of comfort yet," she laughs, "then again after my last hospital stay my posterior is on the sorer side. Now are you ready for my advice?"

I nod. "Yes, but first Gladys, I need to know what's been happening to you?" And I'm sure she would have told me about the emergency surgery, Boat Club staff visits and her slight crush on the consultant if Dizzy hadn't come over to the table. "I haven't had a chance to say this before, but today you were amazing on the water," I say admiringly, because even if she's won the business contest I'm still intrigued to want to know, "how did you get to be so good?"

"Well it took a long time but I was at university in Southampton with this woman called Holly Pye," explains Dizzy, one hand on her mum's shoulder. " You might have heard of Holly as she's a British paddleboard racer, very skilled and very fast. We were living in the same block in our first year and when she heard that I'd loved to skateboard and kayak as a kid she talked me into coming out on a paddleboard. Long story short, she set up a uni SUP club and I did a lot of practice with her. We had such good times…

"It was very tough leaving uni and coming back to London. If Mami hadn't still had the cleaning job at the Boat Club I don't think I could have coped so far from the ocean. But at the Boat Club it was at least easy to watch over Mami and do some of my Masters module studies and that kept me focused and by water too."

"I thought I was keeping an eye on you," jokes Gladys.

"Everyone knows now, but her heart hasn't been great for a while. It was a secret really, but she had a phase of dizzy spells. They just came on with no warning, and then she'd just tumble over whether she was on the stairs, in the cubicles or by the water. So I liked to be with her, making sure she was upright. But that last trip to A&E just when Jack and I were quarrelling about SUP moves got Mami in front of the right doctor and I think she's got the right blood pressure medicine and treatment now," says Dizzy, forced to end what should be a much longer explanation as Bio Queen calls for hush.

"Wow that's a lot to take in," I whisper.

"I just want to say thank you to everyone who has been part of the *Wholly Shit Show*," says Bio Queen with a big smile, tapping on the portable loud hailer that one of the artists passes her. Amplified her voice could bring the buses on Old Street to a stop or knock graffiti off the canal bridges.

"We've made good progress today at this year's special campaigning Canal Festival and are very glad that the Wild Women swimmers, famous for their Anti Algal Bloom Boom campaign came and lent their support. Over the past few months we've done so many litter picks and water quality surveys, often with the good paddleboarding folk at #OutdoorSisters and it's not only cleaned up Regent's Canal, it's also inspired many of the artists here today. It's all hush hush, but I have a hunch that Martyn and pals will be inviting everyone at today's Trashspiration Canal Festival to his flooded Tate Turbine Hall opening in the not too distant future!"

She pauses to wait for the cheers to subside. Bio Queen definitely knows how to work this friendly crowd. What's more she probably knows everyone who is listening, and what kind of cuppa they prefer, except maybe the social media influencer who lives on TikTok (and takeaways).

"And we've had our ace investigator and podcaster USP grill all sorts, from water company bosses and MPs to manufacturing CEOs, sometimes from the most eccentric of studios – a boat that he moored near our cafe," continues Bio Queen. "It's true that we haven't seen all the changes we want yet, but we will. As my dear, much missed friend, the late great Anita Roddick said, if you don't think something small can make a difference then you haven't slept in a room with a mosquito. Let us all be mosquitoes – or if you prefer visible pieces of shit" – she says this gesturing at the considerable number of people dressed up as big brown turds – "and keep on making sure those in authority learn to care about the damage that's been done by incompetent profiteers…"

At this point the crowd starts to clap again, led by USP, who is standing by the local MP, a blonde woman who looks like an older Flame. If USP is Flame's half-brother, then this older woman must be their mum.

The MP, fanning herself with the latest *Islington Tribune*, moves towards a mic. I should stay and listen but there's only so much of the Flame family show I can take feeling this flustered. At times I've thought everyone but me was about to run #OutdoorSisters, but now I know it's Dizzy, I'm happy for her, but still feel defeated.

I lost. She won.

I tell myself that without Flame's dog to mind, there's not much point staying in this crowd. There's no way I can run taster sessions today. I'm not even sure I can talk to anyone sensibly right now. Instead I'll escape the politicking and congratulating and just go for a paddle. That's the only thing that's ever sorted my head out.

Ellie sees me leave and gives a friendly wave as I sidle out of the Narrowboat Cafe. On a hunch I go to the *Buddleia's* prow in the hope that the paddleboard Jack organised to get me to the podcast earlier is still tied up there.

It is.

Just as I unhook the board's Velcro leash Ellie appears. "Lara, aren't you going to help Dizzy with the paddle tasters?" she asks. "She's definitely going to need us all on board with this big crowd."

"I feel like I've helped her out enough, just by being a bit incompetent," I say sadly.

"You've got it wrong! Dizzy is the absolute best person to run #OutdoorSisters, but for her to make it a success we need to help her too," counters Ellie firmly.

"I get what you're saying," I say trying hard not to cry, "and I will, but I've done enough helping today."

"OK Lara, stay well. We all love you," says Ellie and to prove it she then helps me on to the board and passes me her own, full water bottle. "Stay hydrated in this heat!" she laughs. "See you soon."

•••••

As I paddle feebly off on my knees and away from the Boat Club, the MP and Bio Queen's voices at last crackle out of hearing.

By the Bridge of Sighs, with Ellie's water all drunk, I'm ready to stand.

Just after Sturt's Lock I've got my rhythm, paddle face into the water on the in breath, paddle out with the out breath. As I relax something catches my eye below the board, a flash of light maybe off a quick moving dace fish? Or is it someone's wristwatch that needs rescuing?

Sighing, I turn my board around to recheck, and that's when I see the body.

Oh my, it looks like Greg. In his favourite shirt.

How can Greg be dead in this canal if he's run away to India?

21. LOCK LESS MONSTER

Lara needs help

Every part of me wants to panic. But I know what to do if you find a dead body because it's a question I Googled after one of my early paddles with #OutdoorSisters. Basically we had to paddle over five firemen working with two divers in the shallow water near the Bridge of Sighs. For the rest of the trip all the paddleboarders talked about was what they would do if they unexpectedly found a body, laughing even as the hair stood up on the back of our necks, because no one likes being in a horror story. Back home I checked what was recommended.

It did get awkward when Greg, taking a break from watching Arsenal Invincibles on Prime, found our shared laptop left open on What To Do With a Dead Body? The memory swings back vividly, perhaps because he was wearing that same shirt, red and white check from Charles Tyrwhitt.

> *Me: (Looking up from laptop search) Do you want a cup of tea?*
> *Greg: It's 9pm! Why would I want tea? You know I've never drunk tea.*
> *Me: Sorry, I was busy on the laptop. I didn't mean PG tips anyway, just peppermint leaves from the garden or something.*
> *Greg: Homegrown peppermint! Are you trying to poison me?*

Me: Oh, I hadn't thought of that.
Greg: (Looking over my shoulder at the screen).
He reads aloud slowly:

> **"What Should You Do if You Find a Dead Body?**
>
> - **Do not touch anything. This could be a situation where a crime has occurred.**
> - **Call 999.**
> - **Ensure your safety.**
> - **Cooperate with medical professionals and police.**
> - **If it's your responsibility to clean up, strongly consider getting professional assistance."**

Greg: (Deadpan) You really are trying to get rid of me now that you've discovered boring me to death with your unappealling love of paddleboarding isn't working. I can tell you what you call the partner of a paddleboard obsessive, paddle-bored. I'm not joking either.
Me: (Flustered) It's not what you think. Look, there are 15,320,000,000 answers to the question on Google. Lots of people want to know what to do if you find a dead body, didn't you hear me talking at dinner about my SUP today with the firemen doing a search and rescue in the water beneath us?
Greg: (Walking away) No. I'm not in the habit of listening to you blather on about your canal universe. It's small, dull and pointless.

Me: (says nothing, but I remember feeling that in all likelihood my husband now rates Tottenham higher than me).

Turns out my internet search info is useful. But my mind is in turmoil. Could Greg have fallen into the canal on that awful June night he left and no one's noticed? While selfish me just thought he'd done a runner and didn't tell anyone he was missing. Poor, poor Greg. I know that I need to ring 999. I know I have to tell the police.

But when I look for my phone, padding desperately around the waist pocket on my leggings for a bulge, it's missing. I must have left it in Pericles' dog bag, so it's not lost.

But it's not with me.

I try and take a bearing, so that I'll be able to find this awful spot again. The canal is really wide in this bit and there's a weir making a little waterfall to the side of the lock which stirs things up. But there is a yellow barge moored on the far side so I suppose the body – Greg – is in line with its third port hole and the litter bin by the bench on the towpath side. I take a deep breath, shout the word "calm" at myself, then position my board over 'it', trying very hard not to look too closely. I'd like to unsee those staring eye sockets. That ugly, bloodless pallor will haunt me for life.

I try to concentrate as I count my paddle strokes back to the towpath and help. One, two, three, four, five, keep counting, keep breathing calmly, up to 16 and I'm back at the towpath. I've got the coordinates the best I can. I struggle off my board and cry great drops of horror. And outrage. And shock. Greg and I had good times too. How could I have just given up when he went off without saying goodbye?

"What could possibly be the matter, Lara?" says a man pulling up with a squeal of bike brakes. "You're actually bawling, like a child. Surely you can't be that upset by Dizzy taking over #OutdoorSisters? Personally I'm relieved, I never had time to run it the way Flame would have liked, and that was from the get go, way before she started demanding spreadsheets and cash injections."

It's Jack! Capable, wonderful, irritating Jack. I have never been so pleased to see someone so annoying as I am right now.

Chokingly I say hi and try to explain I've lost my phone and... there's a body in the canal.

"A body in the canal?" he says slowly, beginning to understand my tears.

"Is the body dead?" he asks focusing towards where I'm pointing.

"Yes! It looks awful, like it's been there for months. And please don't keep saying that word, 'body'," I snuffle.

"Why? Are you thinking if I do, that everyone will want one?" he says cracking a totally inappropriate, and unfunny, joke.

"It's not just a body. It's Greg."

"It's always this bit of the canal where we seem to lose the clients," says Jack, still in funny mode. "Seriously though, remind me who's Greg?"

"He's my husband."

"Wow," mutters Jack stepping closer to me as I wobble on the canal edge. The blood seems to be surging in and out of my ears, like tide in the narrows, but I hear Jack say calmly, "OK, got that, Greg's your husband. Um, when did you last see him?"

"About three months ago. He told me that he was going to India, and left suddenly. He's never contacted me since then," I confess and collapse in a semi faint on to the towpath sobbing.

Jack sits down beside me, both of us with our backsides on the ground and our feet on my board. He leans my head forward, puts an arm around me and gives me a couple of choices.

"We need to call the police. But I can see you are really overwrought, so I'm going to ask, do you think we can both paddle out to where you saw the 'body', sorry, Greg, and show me. Not to be nasty, but you do have a habit of not quite seeing what the rest of us are seeing. I think we need to check the site first," he says in a voice that makes it totally clear he doesn't believe a word of what I'm saying.

But he's got a point. Let's double check what I saw.

"We've only got one board," I panic. "I can't go back there again on my own."

"It's alright Lara," says Jack using the same soothing voice he used to help Natasha on the disastrous sunset paddle. "We'll go together."

He tells me to get on to the board a bit further forward than normal, while he takes over my paddle and kneels behind me. "Captain Lara, use your best navigational skills please," he says in his most officious voice while starting to paddle in the direction that I'm pointing.

I count out 16 paddle strokes, and look down, there's nothing, or we've overshot.

Jack, looking intently into the canal, spins the board round slowly and then gives a gasp. "My God you were right, there is something monstrous in the water. And it is a body, or at least bits of one." He leans over the shape and removes his sunglasses to double check.

"Does Greg have two arms?" he asks stupidly.

"Of course," I say.

"Well he doesn't now. And Lara, steal yourself because he doesn't have any legs either."

I give a gasp, totally unable to process what Jack's saying. All summer I thought Greg had abandoned me, I even gave his signed Arsenal shirts to the charity shop. How wrong could I be?

Shuddering, I try not to watch as Jack fishes around with the paddle to find a way of drawing up Greg's horribly mutilated body.

I feel dizzy thinking about how maybe he fell into the lock after going for a drink. I imagine the worst, maybe he cried out and no one heard? Or hit his head then drowned? Since then he must have swashed around this canal, rotting. Been repeatedly hit by barge propellers. Gnawed at by fish. Had his liver pecked away by the diving cormorants.

"Shut your eyes, I don't want you to faint properly," says Jack while I'm squeaking about how we need to call the police, right now. But I do what he says and keep my eyes totally glued together as Jack lays something heavy and dripping behind me, and in front of him. The board sinks a little under the weight.

"There's three of us now," says Jack, paddling us back to the towpath.

For a while I cannot move. Instead I just listen to Jack rustling around, dragging the body off my paddleboard. "I think it's OK to look now," says Jack eventually, "but you're in for a big shock."

Instead I put out my hand for him to hold, which he takes, kindly. "Now Lara, do you know anyone who knows Greg's phone number, seeing as you haven't got your phone," he says.

"I think my friend Adebola will have it. She's known us both for years."

"I'm not sure who Adebola is when she's at home," says Jack, puzzled. "Anyone else?"

"I'm always talking about Adebola because she's tall, black and beautiful but won't SUP with me – or answer her phone." This seems a strange conversation to be having with Jack in such a dark moment.

"Oh, the woman Slimeon, sorry USP, was hanging around with today. I think I'll call him, she was with him when I left about half an hour ago."

There are some muffled phone noises and then presumably USP answers. Jack asks if Adebola is with him and could he speak to her. There's more muffling and the phone seems to be handed on. "I'll just put you on speaker," says Jack firmly. "Now listen Adebola I don't know you, but I'm with a very, very upset Lara who says she hasn't seen her husband Greg all summer. Do you know where he is?"

Adebola gives a mock snort (she was always good at sounding pissed off) and says, "Well I hope she's miserable for snogging my fiancé. But yes, I do know where Greg is as he's been hiding in our friend Tim's flat. He's definitely alive and well, just trying to avoid his boring, paddleboard-obsessed wife."

Jack sniffs as if surprised by her tone, but then asks, "Do you think he might have thrown himself in the canal, in a suicidal way since you last saw him?"

"Not a chance," says Adebola with complete confidence, "he was with Tim this morning and they were going to watch Arsenal play. They'll be at the match now, and they're two-nil up. I don't think that's going to make Greg want to shuffle off this mortal coil. Why do you ask?"

"I'll explain another time, but thanks. Hope USP's *Wholly Shit Show* is living up to its name," adds Jack ending the call abruptly. He gives my hand a reassuring squeeze. "This is a hard day isn't it? That chat kind of took me by surprise, but 3,2,1, open wide!"

Still feeling nauseous I blink my eyes open, taking a while to adjust to the bright light. As everything slowly comes back into view – the dancing gnats, the dapples on the water, a struggling pineapple weed pushing up through some bits of broken glass – I see that my dead Greg is in fact a shop window mannequin painted mostly a metallic blue, apart from a blotchy patch of red and white which I mistook for checks. He's in a terrible mess, leaking canal water from his armpits. Confused, I turn him over, dislodging a couple of water leaches.

"It's not Greg," I stutter, relieved.

Jack doesn't actually laugh at this moment. He will repeatedly in the future when retelling the story of the day Lara mistook a shop dummy in the canal for her husband.

"I'm really glad Greg's not dead, and that we didn't call the police, because I think it would have been mortifying for us both," he says, bringing me back to the present by removing my hand from the mannequin. "I know I'm not good on empathy but I do think you've got a bit of life laundry to sort out. And why's your friend Adebola being so horrible? She was bang out of order," says Jack, handing me a satsuma that he seems to have found in his shorts pocket. "More importantly I think you need to get your blood sugar up, for the shock. Hopefully this won't give you the same reaction as that brownie, I really couldn't cope with you going 'crazy girl' again."

I feel so sick from everything that's happened in the past half hour that I'm not sure eating even a segment of satsuma could be possible, but then I relent, taste it and very soon start to feel better. The banging tension in my head drops off and my breath starts to slow down. Very soon there's nothing but pith and skin left in my hand. Jack takes this from me and pops it back into his pocket.

"Why's your friend not like you?" he asks.

"Oh she was never like me," I say, misunderstanding. "She was always going out and being the archetypal good time girl. She loves dressing up and booking restaurants, that kind of thing," I say. I feel as if I've been out of my body and I'm gradually coming home.

Jack laughs. "What I meant was what's gone wrong between you, it seems like there's some bad blood."

"Well she's the sporty one – we've known each other since college – but when I got into paddleboarding last year she just found it quite tame. Boring I guess. And, well you heard her, she'd say all I talked about now was paddleboarding. While you lot at the Boat Club think I don't have a clue."

"Oh come on Lara, I'm sure even you abbreviated SUP and asked her to sup-per. That would be a red flag for anyone," says Jack clearly trying to lighten the mood. His annoying pun brings me squarely back to being me. I see there's a moorhen on the water and a fisherman by the graffiti-covered weir. My feet feel soaking.

A couple of runners thump past trailing a mix of sweat and floral antiperspirant.

"Jack, I've kept you a bit long, sorry. You must have been on some kind of mission on your bike and you stopped to help, thank you. And well you've actually rescued me, totally. It hadn't clicked how some of the people who should have been supporting me, didn't. And some of the ones who I didn't think did, in fact, all of you #OutdoorSisters, well, you really do have my back. It's just I hadn't noticed. I guess I was wrapped up in my messy problems. I'm sorry. Thank you."

"Captain Lara, there's no need to thank any of us. You're a sweetie, perhaps you need to get a bit grittier to survive this cruel world," says Jack, rather poetically. "Actually you are right, I've got to go now, so if you're up to returning that paddleboard to the Boat Club could you? My tip is to then go find your friends. I mean Flame and Ellie and Dizzy and Gladys as they'll all be with Bio Queen. I'm going to give them a heads up," he says pulling out his phone again. "And maybe just stay clear of USP and Adebola today. You can sort the Greg problem out another time, especially as you've managed to leave it for months already. But I do want to give you a little gift, just because I know you need some love right now."

I look quizzically at Jack as he tells me what this gift is, imagining what the neighbours will think when they see a rodent exterminator van parked outside my home. But Jack's right, his gift is just what I need. He's promising to charm away the mice in my home and is sending someone over ASAP.

From tomorrow I'm going to be able to sleep again.

22. NOT A RIPPLE DISTURBS THE WATER

Back with the Boat Club crew: Lara, Jack, Ellie, Gladys and Dizzy

Summer might be over, but it's followed by an October season when mist steams off the water as the sun fights to wake up. I turn over, eyes half shut against the low slanting rays, then exhale as my board drifts through the curtain of yellow willow leaves to a secret spot hidden not far from the big long Angel tunnel. This is my happy place – an autumn domed room where I can break rules (though I can no longer tie my leash to the NO MOORING sign after that little incident in the summer), and relax, out of view of the opposite towpath and out of the way of any early boats using the nearby City Road lock.

It feels nice again to be on my own, away from the stress of divorce papers but at least Greg has apologised for his moonlight flit. To be fair we were in increasingly different spaces: mine was this canal, his Arsenal.

I close my eyes and quietly trail my fingers in the deep water listening out for the coot family that lives nearby. All is peace until there's a rustle and bump as someone else nudges their board into this little hidden space.

I sit up sharply, but rather too much to the left side and overbalance.

Plop. I'm in this canal, again. After all the sewage talk at the Canal Festival, I've learnt to keep my mouth shut.

I'm also sensibly clad in my orange drysuit, just in case. Not that I ever let on why I had to buy it.

"I'm not sure you've really understood how to paddleboard, it's more about standing up, but maybe you're just looking for another supermarket trolley," laughs the voice leaning closer to me. Despite all his campaigning podcasts USP doesn't seem to have any personal concerns about sewage in the water.

I sink quickly out of his reach, having learnt the hard way never to trust him, before channelling my inner seal so I can kick up a froth of bubbles and, half-slither back on to my board, hair dripping, woolly hat lost.

Despite this summer's battle for Flame's paddleboard business, my self-rescue has no chance of being called elegant. But who cares? No one on Regent's Canal. In the distance I can hear the London traffic, the kids starting their day at the Boat Club, even the hiss of a barista coffee being prepped at the *Buddleia* Narrowboat Cafe. Somebody's dog barks as the lock gates clank shut.

All at once the calm dissolves as three more paddleboarders turn up: Ellie, Dizzy and Jack.

"What's s-up," shouts Jack, trying his new, most grating, greeting. "I've brought the office to you seeing as you seem to have forgotten we had a breakfast meeting today. Dizzy's got a SUP proposition for you. And we needed her financial angel, USP, to be here too."

I definitely don't remember any breakfast meeting in the calendar.

USP beams. "I thought Adebola and I did well making sure Lara was in the right place this morning. Actually before you all start pontificating, I'd like to officially replace the flask that Lara lost here when she famously got stuck in a supermarket basket due to my crashing lack of stand-up paddleboard skill. Thanks to you all I'm better now. And so without further ado the good news is that Bio Queen found your missing flask when she was trying to demonstrate to the men in suits at the Canal & River Trust how much this bit of canal needs a dredge," he says handing over a beaten up, rusty cylinder that might have been my old Thermos. But might not. "I also want to say sorry to you Dizzy, in public, again, for the many times I've offended you. I think we agreed I was to do this at least once a day for a year."

"Yes," says Dizzy, rolling her eyes. Then she addresses me rather more sensibly. "The thing is Lara, we definitely need you full time at #OutdoorSisters. You see Jack wants to go paddleboard racing this winter. So he's taking his PT with him, and of course that's Ellie, and now she wants to do the same races, so her plan is to get Jack to time her when he's not building up muscle, driving the van or moonlighting as the Pied Piper with his revolting vermin exterminator trade. As for me, I can't bear to think of wasting another lifetime – well winter – not racing, when I could be, so my financial backer has encouraged me to join them. Which means…"

Dizzy looks at me, hoping perhaps that I'll figure it out.

"It's all about the sup-reme sacrifice," says Jack happily.

"Which means?" I ask, clutching the battered Thermos. I'm confused about what she's getting at.

"Well Lara, as I'm the boss," she laughs happily, "I've got a proposal, like Jack and USP said, and I hope you'll love it. You see I'd really like you to take on #OutdoorSisters this winter, but still work for us next summer. As you know after Easter I've got a heap of plans for club swaps, community days, treat trips, tours, skills and drill sessions, you name it, but that's for when the weather is warmer. But as we go into winter we just need to offer SUP and chat for our regulars at the Boat

Club who love going up and down the canal, even in the cold. And we need them to stay safe.

"Lara, I want you to run that," she adds to make sure I understand.

Ellie brings her board alongside mine and gives me a huge smile. I can see her fingers are crossed, hopefully, where they are resting on the paddle shaft. "None of us can actually go racing unless you're willing to take over the winter weekend work," she whispers.

The calm sanctuary of a few moments ago might be gone, but in its place is an offer that can only have one answer. "Yes. Yes, please!"

I give Dizzy a hug. Then Ellie. Then Jack. And a little wave to USP. "If this is a really 'real' offer then thank you, every single one of you, for following your dreams so I get to live my best life, right here. Now. please let's go and celebrate with a coffee at the *Buddleia* Narrowboat Cafe before anyone changes their mind," I say.

"We thought that's what you'd suggest," says Dizzy, so Mami and Flame are already waiting there. "Bio Queen rejigged the decor this weekend with you in mind. She's actually a bit nervous about what you're going to make of it. Let's go and see," she says paddling off.

But I already know what Bio Queen's done: taken that daft blue mannequin and added it as a figurehead to her boat. It doesn't look like an armless Greg now that it's been sprayed black and gold and plastered with costume jewels. It does have artistically broad shoulders on to which I'm sure people will be invited to sacrifice their jacket. Just for luck I'll leave this rotten Thermos by it. Call it a votive offering or littering, I really don't mind.

It's extraordinary what the universe provides, always with added twists. Four months ago I was lonely, although I'm not sure I knew that. But I'd promised myself a new start and maybe a better bike. One out of two isn't a bad result, and honestly who needs a new bike when someone like Jack is able to fix just about anything? I've also found my tribe, with the very same people who at the start of the summer I'd thought were my mortal rivals.

As our little group paddles towards latte, Americanos, cake, churros and paddleboard plans I look back to the willow bower and the broken 'No Mooring' sign. Already the coots are regrouping, and I can see there's not a ripple disturbing the water, but a giant wave of good fortune.

Exactly how I felt when Flame offered me the most exciting project of my life.

THE END

BOOK GROUP DISCUSSION STARTERS

1 Have you (or a friend) adopted a new habit or sport which you can't stop talking about? For Lara it was paddleboarding, but it could be a no sugar diet, 5:2 fasting, veganism, wild water swimming, pilates? How does that make your old friends and family feel?

2 In the book there are a number of accidental pet deaths which make Jack look cruel, especially when you discover that his other job is as a rodent exterminator – but he eats a vegetarian diet. Thinking critically, do you think that humans are inconsistent about their treatment of animals and wildlife?

3 Lara ends the novel with friends of all ages. How important are shared hobbies in cementing friendships?

4 Paddleboard owner Flame is in control at all times and with all people, but having a puppy changes this. Do you think she was prepared for this complication?

5 This novel focuses on a tiny geographical area in London along a short stretch of Regent's Canal. Does knowing a place really well make it bigger or smaller? What other books (and writers) that you've read are linked to place?

6 Hegel is a 19th century German philosopher adopted by the political Left and Right. Looking at some of the Hegel

quotes in the book do you feel they shed insight on to contemporary problems, or were they just a way for USP/Simon to look clever or stupid (depending on your own viewpoint)? Do you or friends/family have catchphrases that get rolled out a little too often? Why?

7 Jack loves a pun. Did you enjoy the use of sup-er puns in the novel? Do you think this device is used to stop readers realising that Jack is basically a solid nice bloke? Are there tics, haircuts or even clothing that you find make you dismiss people, regardless of their actions?

8 The story is told from Lara's point of view. Does this make her your favourite character or does someone else earn that honour? Why?

9 In what ways do young people have it different to older generations? Lara seems convinced that she's having an unfair ride into her 50s but she's a Baby Boomer (eg, she has a mortgage for a house rather than renting a flat). What do you think about comparing generational cohorts? Is it a useful temperature-take or a reductionist insult?

10 Does the novel make you want to do more exploring of your local waterway? Or have a go on a paddleboard? Or perhaps it reminded you of a time when you did try paddling? What made you stop?

Thank you for reading NOT THAT DEEP. If you would like to review it please go ahead as this is a great way to help share and publicise the book.

ALSO BY NICOLA BAIRD

Nicola Baird is an environmental journalist, blogger and author. She's also a stand-up paddleboard coach (with BSUPA and Paddle UK) and was a #ShePaddles ambassador in 2024. If you enjoyed reading NOT THAT DEEP, you might also like her other books and websites which mostly focus on environmental non-fiction topics or interviews.

Why Women Will Save the Planet (ed)
Homemade Kids
Islington Faces 2013
Save Cash & Save the Planet (with Andrea Smith)
A Green World?
The Estate We're In: who's driving car culture?
Coconut Wireless (novel)
How to Make & Use Visual Aids (with Nicola Harford)
Setting Up & Running a School Library

*****

www.islingtonfacesblog.com

https://nicolabairdtalkssup.substack.com

https://aroundbritainnoplane.blogspot.com

Printed in Great Britain
by Amazon